OUTERMOST

SHADOW OF THE DOMINION: BOOK 3

BLAZE WARD

KNOTTED ROAD PRESS

Outermost
Shadow of the Dominion: Book 3
Blaze Ward
Copyright © 2019 Blaze Ward
All rights reserved
Published by Knotted Road Press
www.KnottedRoadPress.com

ISBN: 978-1-64470-083-9

Cover art:

ID 25360826 © Philcold | Dreamstime.com

Cover and interior design copyright © 2019 Knotted Road Press

Never miss a release!
If you'd like to be notified of new releases, sign up for my
newsletter.

I will never spam you, or use your email for nefarious purposes.
You can also unsubscribe at any time.

http://www.blazeward.com/newsletter/

Shadow of the Dominion

Longshot Hypothesis

Hard Bargain

Outermost

Dominion-427

Phoenix

Princess Rualoh

The Jessica Keller Chronicles

Auberon

Queen of the Pirates

Last of the Immortals

Goddess of War

Flight of the Blackbird

The Red Admiral

St. Legier

Winterhome

Petron

CS-405

Queen Anne's Revenge

Packmule

Persephone

Additional Alexandria Station Stories

The Story Road

Siren

Two Bottles of Wine with a War God

The Science Officer Series

The Science Officer

The Mind Field

The Gilded Cage

The Pleasure Dome

The Doomsday Vault

The Last Flagship

The Hammerfield Gambit

The Hammerfield Payoff

Earth Force Sky Patrol

Birth of the Star Dragon

Flight of the Star Dragon

Call of the Star Dragon

Shadow of the Star Dragon

Trial of the Star Dragon

Other Science Fiction Stories

Myrmidons

Moonshot

Menelaus

Earthquake Gun

Moscow Gold

Fairchild

White Crane

The Collective Universe
The Shipwrecked Mermaid
Imposters

[1]
GLAXU

WELL, that sucked. Nothing could be done to fix this ship, either. At least not with the parts available on this stupid, forgotten planet, that was sure.

Glaxu considered kicking something in frustration, but he'd either break whatever was his target, or his foot. And it would never do for him to be as lamed as his fightership. He let the profanities roll out of his beak as a distant second choice to keeping the rage inside his head.

Not that he hadn't brought this on himself. His ship was named *Outermost* for a reason. Always the widest ship on the combat wing of the formation, closest to the enemy. At least, back when he flew with the rest of his nest and they were the scourge of the spaceways.

How many months had it actually been since he had even seen another Mondi warrior? Six? Eight?

Glaxu closed the housing over the left-hand engine's injector coils carefully and cursed some more. He'd been so close! Now he was stuck on this damned planet until someone came along that could fix his warp array. Good luck, when the stupid, hairless monkeys that dominated this sector could barely make a warpbubble in the first place, let alone something as sophisticated as a Southern Chain.

The ones on this planet were even worse, such a weird collection of shapes and colors that somehow all got classified as human, regardless of everything else. Incompetents and barbarians, the lot of them. And the next human that called him a roadrunner to his beak was getting arteries ripped out with a dewclaw. He didn't care if they were two or three times his size. Their balance was all wrong anyway, and they were practically harmless if they didn't have a knife or a beam weapon in their hands when they started getting mouthy.

How had those worthless shits managed to conquer or colonize most of known space with their eggs?

Trick question, they had always been here, and the Mondi had only started to explore this section of the galaxy in the last eleven lifetimes. Just long enough to settle in, and get himself separated from his nest when his warpstream chain failed mid-flight, dropped him off the formation, and left him here.

Rooters. Sentient bastards with their heads nevertheless stuck in the ground.

Glaxu gave up and kicked his toolbox with an outer toe as he went by. Not enough to break anything, just skid it across the deck a little in frustration. He could head forward and maybe check the cockpit of *Outermost*, but he already had his personal radio programmed to receive signals from the ship, if anybody capable of real technology actually happened along.

Pink, blue, purple, or green humans notwithstanding.

Grumbling, he gripped the wooden deck with all eight toes for a moment and then pivoted aft. Through the rear airlock and down the ramp to the sand where he had sat *Outermost* down when it was clear he was lost.

Before he realized he was also trapped on this planet with several tribes of xenocidal monkeys still amazed by indoor plumbing, to say nothing of electricity. Okay, maybe that last one wasn't fair. Those killers were right on the bleeding edge of sophistication when it came to modern weaponry.

It was only their social organization that left much to be desired. At least they had left him alone after he had killed three of them in personal duels. Idiots thought bulk made them impressive, fighting someone half their size, a tenth their weight, and twice their brains. With built-in dewclaws.

So he had ended up moving *Outermost* into the deep desert to try and fix the ship. At least it reminded him of the home he wasn't going to see anytime soon. And they even had several species of snakes native on this planet, so he'd never go hungry or lack for entertainment. Better, since the dumb snakes didn't see him as a predator.

Kinda like the stupidly-large humans.

The sun was extremely hot, even for him. This place probably never should have been colonized, regardless of your need. Mondi as a species liked heat, whereas most of the human derivatives got even less capable after being out in it for a while.

But they'd fought a huge war here at some point. The whole sector, and not just this planet. Something called the Urlan Empire had claimed most of what everyone called Wildspace now. Back when it was supposedly civilized.

He'd also known enough Urlans in his time to put paid to that silliness as well. Those people were only polite when you had a gun on them, or a dewclaw resting on a throat.

Glaxu looked up, but nothing had changed since yesterday in this remote valley where he had landed. He walked over to the chair he had unfolded, adjusted his squatting cloth, and dropped down into it to think. Somewhere on this planet were folks who could get him off of it. Or at least find the parts he needed to fix his ship. He could limp someplace more civilized at that point, and then find his way to…

Where? He'd wanted to stay in this sector when the rest of the nest had voted to head for home instead. Or at least where there were a few Mondi. Didn't have to be home. That might take years, but over yonder. Losing his warp bubble coils hadn't improved his humor.

Sounded no more appetizing now than it had then. He needed a new nest. Which would be a trick, when he might be the only Mondi left in this sector. Maybe this octant, depending on how fast everyone else moved, once they got their Southern Chain linked up and pushing.

Crap.

And he'd hunted out all the snakes dumb enough to live around here, at least until more moved in.

Maybe he'd go hunting tomorrow for something to do.

A beep broke his concentration.

Damn it, now what's broken?

But it wasn't another engine warning signal. None of those beeped politely. They were programmed to make obnoxious noises until you reset them or fixed whatever had gone wrong when you decided to push the damned envelope a little too far.

Like usual.

Glaxu looked around, craning his long neck until he realized that the sound was coming from one of the pockets on his bandolier. He stared at it kind of cross-eyed down his beak for a second, and then stuffed a hand into the pouch and pulled out the radio unit.

Well, duh.

He opened the channel, but whoever it was had stopped transmitting. Or passed over the horizon. But Praise The Gods, someone had come.

Now he just needed to sweet talk these sentients out of some parts to fix his warp engine.

Or steal them.

[2]
VALENTINIAN

"ALL HANDS, this is your illustrious and overly-awesome captain speaking," Valentinian said as he opened an intercom line and let everyone hear his voice.

Just 'cause, ya know? They'd all been behaving reasonably well, including Bayjy, who he figured would probably be the most stir-crazy at this point. Dave was quiet even at his loudest. Kyriaki was…

She was still a cop. He had a hard time getting past that point, even if she was as much a fugitive with a price on her head as he was. Maybe more, since she was also now a traitor to the Dominion's Security Bureau. The White Hats.

Dave was just the man who many suspected as having assassinated the previous Dominator, a new one having finally been crowned by now, even if they were so far from Cronus Prime that the news would be months getting here. Valentinian was merely the criminal scum who had helped the assassin escape from justice several times. But Kyriaki used to be a cop. The one chasing he and Dave.

Before she saved their lives. Again. And pissed off Dave's now-ex-wife, the representative of the Dominion Household itself, the woman sworn to chase them up to and through the gates of hell itself. And, according to Dave, she was the sort of woman who would do exactly that.

Which left Bayjy. She was the most innocent one here, but that wouldn't protect her if they did end up getting caught. Everyone would go under a good dose of truth serum, and none of them would ever come out the far side.

Or worse, they might. On Cronus Prime.

"Did you have news, or just wanted to make sure we were all awake?" Bayjy layered the sarcasm on like a puff pastry over the internal radio. She was good at that. "Some of us might have been napping."

"Oh, well far be it for me to interrupt that," Valentinian replied. "But if you opened an appropriately-facing porthole, you might notice that we just dropped out of warp over Kryuome."

Checking his boards, she had been in her cabin up a deck, but he heard her racing across the steel deck and pounding down the stairs at a high rate of speed, getting closer like an avalanche. Fortunately, he had the rear hatch open as she came barreling into the rec space, one step ahead of both Dave and Kyriaki, interestingly enough.

"How is this possible?" Bayjy demanded breathlessly. "According to the sailing directions, we shouldn't be here for at least four more days."

"If it would make you feel better, we could sit in

orbit for a bit, and then land like a regular cargo transport," Valentinian snarked at her.

"Don't you dare!" she said right back with a smile.

Valentinian just grinned. From the surly and occasionally angry salvager he had first met, her irrepressibleness had finally taken hold again. This was probably more like her default setting, before her previous captain had screwed her out of a major payday and then abandoned her on Bohrne Station.

Of course, that man, Butler Vidy-Wooders, captain of the salvage freighter *Hard Bargain*, had gotten his. Bayjy and Kyriaki had snuck aboard his ship and stolen all her gear back, plus the six other storage crates from crew Vidy-Wooders had abandoned, before turning the internal ship's temperature up to forty-five degrees, and then breaking the controls.

As well as spiking open his refrigerator and freezer so all his food spoiled.

That had been the signature move. Bayjy was one of the Variant Humanities known as Pranai. Almost ten centimeters taller than his one hundred eight-five, with muscles in places Valentinian didn't even have places. Bald, save for eyelashes and thin brows, plus almost no body hair at all. No body fat either under light purple skin that was somewhere darker than lavender, but not much.

The Pranai had been genetically engineered by the Urlan millennia ago for work on ultra-hot planets. Bayjy's idea of comfortable was at least forty degrees, sometimes warmer. Among the things she had stolen back had been her heatsuit, a powered body stocking, skin tight, that kept her at whatever temperature she preferred, when Valentinian liked to keep his ship, the *Longshot Hypothesis*, down around eighteen degrees to save on heating bills.

When he had first met Bayjy, he hadn't even been sure it had been a woman at the core of all those layers, sweaters, and sweatshirts. Today she was in simple, black pants that showed off her bottom running up and down stairs. On top, a white shirt sporting red, three-quarter-length sleeves, with a whiskey advertisement on the front, over those inner heatsuit sleeves down to her wrists. Around her neck, something maybe approximating a cravat, just so she didn't have to wear a knit cap all that often.

"Oh?" Valentinian smiled even larger at her. "So you'd like to head down to the planet and maybe enjoy the day a bit?"

Behind her, he could see Dave and Kyriaki grinning as well. Bayjy was irrepressible, but she was so easy to tease.

"Now, mister," Bayjy demanded. "Gimme some sun."

"Coming up," Valentinian said. "You swap with Dave so he can fly."

There was a moment of shuffling around as bodies moved like a chess board. The cockpit of *Longshot Hypothesis* had two seats and just enough room for maybe a third person to stand behind them. From the brief look of surprise on Dave's face, over Bayjy's shoulder, Valentinian guessed that she had rubbed herself against the taller man while sliding by, like a purring cat.

She might have. Stir-crazy and all that.

Nobody on this ship had fooled around, that he was aware. Dave had two kids Valentinian's age, give or take. Mid-twenties, at least, although he hadn't looked them up. Bayjy and Kyriaki were both closer to thirty, if he had to put a number down. Both in fantastic shape only heightened by the need to run up and down stairs on this ship all the time.

While Bayjy was bald and purple, Kyriaki was a Standard Human with brown hair and blue eyes. He had considered it. Come close a few times, before circumstances or other crew had interrupted.

He still wasn't sure if that was a good thing or not. There was something there in her eyes, at least when she didn't think anybody was looking. But he was the captain of this ship, and she was crew, at least for now.

He really didn't need all those troubles as well. If Bayjy was feeling frisky, let her drag Dave into a closet and snog some.

"What's ground control like?" Dave asked as he finally got settled.

"Non-existent," Valentinian replied. "Pinged the ground a few times, but nobody answered anywhere. That fits with what Stephaneria was able to track down about the planet. The war disrupted it and it's never really recovered."

"How bad?" Dave turned and looked at him.

"Spots of radiation here and there suggest someone used big nuclear weapons at some point in the distant past," Valentinian shrugged. "Background radiation is higher than probably safe, if we were going to be here for a year or three. Not planning that, so we'll be okay for now."

"And no planetary government?" Dave seemed aghast at the concept.

But he had also spent twenty-five years leading

the government of the Dominion. Law and order, plus a healthy dose of lunatic warrior monks intent on conquering the entire galaxy, given the chance.

Was it any wonder the man had suffered a mid-life-crisis, faked his own death, and run away?

"None," Valentinian said. "We are out in Wildspace, big guy. Which reminds me."

He turned to look at the two women, both standing at the doorway and looking in expectantly.

"Everyone will be armed from the moment we hit the ground here," Valentinian ordered. "You will take it with you everywhere, including the bathroom and the shower. The law in places like this is what we bring, so don't trust anyone local, even if they are wearing a badge. And shoot to kill if you have to. I will be swapping my shock pistol for a flamer, and I will be adding a shock rod to my gear. I suggest you do the same."

He liked the way Bayjy's always-expressive eyes got really big. Kyriaki grimaced, but nodded. Dave just shrugged, but Valentinian wasn't sure he'd ever met someone as lethally dangerous as Dave Hall. Especially when the man popped out his telescoping baton and wielded it like a sword.

Death was probably jealous. Valentinian had seen Dave kill or cripple four men so fast that two of them died before they started falling over. And without using a cutting edge.

"Dave, you land us," Valentinian said. "Best you get the practice on a rough field. I've marked some coordinates that seem to be a small city, at least from Stephaneria's notes. It's not that close to our final target, but close enough for now to scout the terrain."

"On it," the big guy put his hands on the controls and began nudging the ship onto the right glide path.

Valentinian studied the world below them as they headed in. Dry and brown for the most part. Wide and dangerous wastelands.

Somewhere down there, on the southeastern portion of the hemisphere-spanning big continent, there was supposedly a ship. At least according to the treasure map Valentinian had memorized. The one he won in an honest, crooked poker game.

Now he just had to go find it.

[3]
ATHANASIA

SHE WOULD CHASE them to the ends of the galaxy and beyond, if that was what it took to get her revenge. To see the man who now introduced himself as Dave Hall pay for everything he had done to her.

She could never go back to what had been her palace on Cronus Prime. As Dowager, she might rate a good suite of rooms on Dominion Prime, away from the Household itself and the center of government, but never again would she be a source of power herself.

Better to just never return to the Dominion at all.

Athanasia suspected that the crew of this ship had been given explicit orders to that effect, the kind that might keep them away from home for years as well. Perhaps forever. Idly, she wondered if the captain of *Dominion-427*, the assault courier she had been given, had done something to anger the powers that be, the Solar Party Mandarins, back home.

Perhaps he had been a little too loyal to the old Dominator, rather than the throne? Was sending him off on a wild good chase punishment for some sin he had never admitted to her? Possibly.

For now, it was enough that this ship was armed, and *Longshot Hypothesis*, as far as she could tell, was not. And that Laurentia recognized her diplomatic credentials and dealt with her with politeness.

She missed having the Ambassador who had traveled with her as far as Tartarus. He was a smart man, educated and erudite. The team of White Hats he had left behind were competent, but little more than that. The ship's captain was a bureaucrat so faceless she occasionally startled when he walked into the cabin to speak with her.

And Kyriaki Apokapes…

That woman would burn in hell. Athanasia didn't know how Hall or Tarasicodissa had seduced her away from her duty, but they had. That bullshit about sneaking aboard their ship so she could capture or disable it was, in retrospect, the perfect cover for the Inspector to escape justice, fleeing into Wildspace with her paramours.

Athanasia had a special vengeance planned for Apokapes. She just needed to catch them.

All the way to the edge of the galaxy, and beyond, if necessary.

"Madam, docking is complete," the captain entered her salon and spoke.

Athanasia shook her head to come back to the antiseptic room around her and stood. Too much wool-gathering. It had not been her style, when she was the wife of the Dominator.

Introspection was time wasted that could have been better served in planning. Still, she was here.

"Very good, Captain," she replied.

The man retreated, leaving the hatch open. In the corridor, she could see the Inspector and the man's small team of White Hats, all armed, standing at attention.

They were for show. If she started trouble here, she would never find the clues she needed to track Dave Hall down.

No, this was better served with honey than vinegar.

She checked her clothing. Long white robes edged in green that made often her appear as a statue if she stood perfectly still. Her blond hair was in the traditional twin braids. In official mourning, she wore no makeup, and let the natural paleness of her skin suggest a ghost to strangers.

Or an avenging angel.

Athanasia preceded the troops forward to the docking tunnel. The hatch was already open, and she could see a small group of folks standing in a polite circle, waiting for her.

Not at any sort of formal attention. Laurentia wouldn't do that, and most certainly would not for a representative of their worst enemy, however diplomatic and polite she might be.

Athanasia studied the man at the center of the small group. Tall, perhaps a little taller than her. Lean and rangy, rather than muscled like the men of the Dominion Household. She guessed he was in his sixties, from the short, gray hair peeking out from under a brown cowboy hat, as well as the gray mustache on his chiseled face. Brown eyes focused warily on her as she emerged onto the concourse.

From the way the others stood, this man was in charge. The rest were much younger, three men and two women. Several of them were armed as was the man at the center.

"Ambassador," the man nodded as she got close. "Welcome to Bohrne Station. I am Ramazan Bolat-Nurlan, Sheriff of the station."

Athanasia considered the man. Sheriff was a political role, as well as a law enforcement one. These others might all be deputies, perhaps. One woman she recognized now as the Stationmaster, but that one was also deferring.

"Thank you," she decided to pour on the charm. "My apologies for our earlier gruffness and the misunderstandings that might have resulted. Is there someplace quiet we could retire to?"

She didn't miss the way Bolat-Nurlan's eyes flickered over her shoulder to note the team of White Hats behind her.

"I won't need them, will I?" she asked lightly.

"You will not," the Sheriff allowed.

Athanasia turned to the Inspector in charge.

"You may return to the ship and go off duty for now," she said simply.

Better to put herself at something of a social disadvantage with this man, and let his ego control the situation. Much easier to manipulate most men that way.

The Inspector nodded silently and the entire team marched back up into the ship, leaving her alone.

"Sheriff?" she smiled up at the man.

"We can talk in my office," he decided.

She noted that most of the deputies departed at that point, leaving only one standing a loose sort of guard on the concourse. Probably in case her White Hats decided to sneak out later and cause trouble.

Athanasia had no idea if the captain would give them shore leave, or leave them in barracks. Hopefully, she wasn't going to be here all that long.

The station had not changed since she was last here, before the unfortunate sidetrip to Meskle. A man walking towards her caught her eye, doubly so when his scale became evident.

As they approached to pass, Athanasia realized that the stranger was three meters tall and built like her former husband, all muscles and power. And angry enough to chew nails, from the thunderous look on his face.

She noted a stutter in the Sheriff's step for just the briefest bit. As though he expected problems with the man. But they passed without words and the giant continued on his angry way.

"Trouble?" she asked quietly, coming up beside the man instead of following him.

"Hopefully not for much longer," the Sheriff said. "The man came here from Begzatlari, but didn't find what he was looking for. In another day or so I'm hoping he departs."

"What was he looking for?" Athanasia asked.

She didn't even recognize the species, other than to know that he was one of the so-called Variant Humanities that were more common in Wildspace and exceedingly rare even in Laurentia, and unknown in the Dominion.

The Sheriff cocked a bit of side-eye at her. Perhaps did a bit of math in his head.

"I won't offer to bribe you, Sheriff," she murmured, stepping a notch closer as they walked and twining her arm into his. "But I am happy to pay for useful information. I understand that Laurentia never has enough cash, and I doubt this station is so rolling in trade that it doesn't need more. I didn't bring trade goods, but I do have funds available."

"Information might be more useful than money, Ambassador," he replied after a beat. "I have questions myself that seek answers, and you probably know them."

"Information is even easier then," she smiled and leaned a touch more into the man as they walked. "Those sorts of trades are always the best kind."

The look on his face suggested that he might welcome some sort of physical exchange as well. She may even look forward to that. Her husband had not touched her in several years at this point, and no other man would dare.

Unless they had no idea who she was.

Or didn't care.

Yes, she could certainly trade with this man.

[4]
DAVE

Scum and villainy was an old saying, but Dave had never actually walked into a place that exemplified it so well. Bars like this barely existed in the sort of places he had been while living as the Dominator. Since turning himself into Dave Hall and seeing the galaxy, Valentinian had largely kept them to the mid-range joints and dives.

Scum *or* villainy, he supposed, but never both at the same time.

At least until today.

They had landed on the outskirts of a small city in the middle of a big desert. Maybe five or eight thousand inhabitants, depending how far underground some of those dome-shaped buildings went. It almost reminded him of an ant hive, seeing tunnels and arcades connecting bigger buildings. Probably to keep the sun off you when you had to scurry between buildings.

The daytime heat was savage. Walking in it had been a chore, but Vee apparently understood the weather, and had made Dave add a long robe and a floppy hat over pants plus a thin shirt that was more a tunic cut high on the sides so he could get to either holster. Valentinian wore the same.

Bayjy was stripped to long shorts she had cut down from a pair of cargo pants, and a simple T-shirt, with a messenger bag slung on one hip. And a smile a mile wide as she walked, but she enjoyed this sort of weather.

Had been born for it. Literally.

Maybe Kyriaki hadn't had the worst idea, electing to remain behind and guard the ship, in the cooler air, while the others got a chance to get out and see something other than those same walls. She wouldn't be sweating or swearing nearly as badly as Dave was under his breath.

At least they had made it into a cantina of some sort. A big, ring-shaped bar at the center of the round interior, with four bartenders working it. Two of them were Standard Humans, and he couldn't tell with the other two. Maybe they were Variant Humans, or maybe just aliens that were close enough in form to pass in the dim light. The Dominion had been far too specist to truly accept any sort of aliens, and never kept slaves, so his education on the subject was quite lacking.

There was a band playing on a raised stage, the kind high enough that Dave was only about at eyeball level with the singer's ankles, as tall as he was. They looked mostly human. Vee had found a small booth right up against the stage and the three of them slid in.

In the vids, the person working the floor in joints like this was always somehow a beautiful, nubile, young woman destined to fall madly in love with the loveable scamp of a main character. Considering the hairy, overweight dude that took their drink orders, Dave was just fine only being the sidekick today. Although he doubted that Vee found the man interesting.

But space never turned out like the vids.

Bayjy just smiled.

"We likely to see any action during the day?" Dave asked.

Evening would be when folks were active. Cool enough to move around comfortably, but not the bitter cold you might get by dawn.

"Only if they're serious," Vee replied, looking somehow utterly casual and ridiculously solemn at the same time.

Dave had never quite figured out how the man did that, but he didn't have to. Valentinian might have been born with that natural charisma. Dave had just needed the man's help to escape.

Several times.

Big, fat, and hairy delivered plastic mugs of thin beer, took some cash, and left them alone. The band was more enthusiastic than skilled, but about what you could expect in a joint like this, on a planet like this, on the left-hand side of Wildspace from the more civilized sectors.

Maybe he'd just gotten too jaded after watching the professionals of Solaria Femina working. Even as teenage girls, they had things down tight. This was a jam band. Dave wasn't even sure they were all playing the same song right now.

His instincts had gotten honed, however, by living a more personally-dangerous life as Dave Hall than he ever had before in his Dominator armor. He spotted the man the instant he came through the door.

Vee had once suggested that they were all cousins, the men and women who worked every spaceport as fixers, finders, or scroungers. It seemed like every one of them had that same, vaguely-oily sheen about them, like you wanted to take a shower after talking to them.

The stranger had that look. Walked in the door, scanned the place, and locked in hard on Vee. Not hard enough that Dave felt the need to come up with a heavy pistol, but that was about the only option more serious. Everyone in this bar was armed to some degree or another. Opening fire would just unleash a semi-apocalyptic shitshow, even if most of them probably didn't even train as hard and accurately as Valentinian did, to say nothing of the standards Dave maintained.

His Caelon assault troopers had been the best in the galaxy. Dave could still outshoot most of them.

Fixer over there seemed to take that into account as he approached. Maybe the negligent smile Dave had on his face. The kind that said it might just be easier to kill you and steal your watch than to stop and ask the time.

The approaching stranger was positively friendly by the time he got close enough to smile at them. Usually they had to sit down before the *bonhomie* came out.

"May I sit?" the man asked with a decidedly odd accent as he stood close. The vowels were too long and the consonants too sharp. Usually you got one, or the other, but not both.

"Selling anything I want to buy?" Valentinian asked laconically.

"What is it you might be in need of?" Fixer asked.

"You came here," Valentinian rumbled. "I didn't come looking for you."

"Indeed, sir," Fixer said, finding his footing finally after Vee knocked him back a stride. "You are strangers here. I have not seen an Anuradhan cargo transport like that in more than a decade."

Dave was just amazed that the man even knew what *Longshot Hypothesis* was. His troops had only finally taken Anuradha about five years ago, and it was on the far side of the Dominion from Wildspace. Call it three thousand light-years from here, minus a little.

"And?" Vee snapped at the stranger.

"So one would expect that you are seeking cargo to transport," the oily butterball said.

Somehow, they were always slightly overweight as well, as though good eating and not enough exercise was part of the job description.

"Kryuome even have anything worth exporting?" Valentinian scowled hard at the man.

Others in here were largely ignoring the conversation. And Vee had not asked the man to sit. Good to know that folks tended towards that level of insularity.

"I'm sure we can find something of interest," the stranger smarmed. "If nothing else, the arms import business never flags."

"Import?" Vee asked, somewhat negligent.

Dave didn't lean into the conversation, but he focused a bit more of his concentration on it. And split the rest looking for someone making a sudden move to either join the conversation or halt it. Ramazan Bolat-Nurlan, the Sheriff of Bohrne Station, might be the only person Dave had ever met as fast with a drawn weapon as he was, but there were probably others out there.

"The mutant tribes of the central belt are forever at war with one another," Fixer opined negligently. "And preying on strangers wandering into that zone. Used gear can always be found at a good price, and they are forever seeking more and better with which to either kill their neighbors or hold their own territory."

Vee grunted. Near as Dave could tell, that had been the first useful thing the man had said, the rest being blather.

"Not buying or selling anything right this moment," Valentinian said finally. "Leave a card and I might give you a call in a few days."

That seemed sufficient. The man dipped into a pocket and produced something that looked like off-white plastic, about six by ten centimeters.

"I look forward to dealing, Captain," he nodded and departed with a jaunty step.

Dave scored it about a draw, which was probably Valentinian's point. *We aren't desperate for anything, nor do we need a gig right now.*

More mysterious that way. At least for the moment

"Now what?" Bayjy spoke up when they were truly alone again.

"Now I need maps," Vee replied quietly. "And maybe some better firepower and a short-range ground transport. You'll need cutting tools and general salvager gear. Hopefully, the thing on the map still exists and hasn't been looted in the last however-long since it was made. I'm guessing we aren't the first prospectors to come along."

"Trouble?" she asked.

"According to the coordinates on that map, where we need to go is somewhere along the central belt," Vee said with a shrug. "Where these apparent mutant tribes are living. What I don't have is the correct zero point to calculate longitude from, and so we have twenty-seven thousand miles of equator to look at, by nearly four degrees of width. Not even a dedicated survey ship is likely to find something in less than several years of looking."

"Gotcha," Bayjy nodded back. "At least it will be good to be out in the sun, finally."

Dave smiled at her and sipped his beer. She had no idea what violence was really like. From what that fixer had intimated, it was a warzone where his Caelons might have troubles. Or fun. At least until they decided to just wipe out everyone instead of going through the effort of pacifying them.

He didn't have that option this time, probably, so they might have to do it one fool at a time.

[5]
RAMAZAN

As Sheriff of Bohrne Station, Ramazan's job was keeping the peace. Not just on his deck, but also in his corner of Laurentia, and sometimes beyond. Anything that threatened that had to be dealt with.

This tall, blond, so-called Ambassador from the Dominion might as well have had *Threat* tattooed on her skin. She was like one of those insects where the bright colors are there as a warning to predators that they are poisonous. Toxic. Whatever the term was.

Lethal.

She had adjusted her persona by the time he got her into his office and got the door closed. Gone was the hard woman filled with bluster, cash, and demands. Something softer had taken up residence instead.

Ramazan had no doubts that the former was more likely to be her actual personality, but he could adapt as well. It wasn't as though she was going to be around long.

If she really wanted to seduce him for information

that a few hours digging in a computer system elsewhere might uncover, who was he to argue? She was not an unattractive woman, if you liked them tall and muscular.

He had been a widower long enough to appreciate all kinds.

"When last you were here…" Ramazan began as they settled.

"When last I was here, I did things in an unfortunate, undiplomatic manner, Sheriff," she cut him off politely but seriously.

Not a woman going for half-measures today.

"Oh?"

"*Longshot Hypothesis* was here and I let my anger get the better of me," she said, leaning back into her chair in a way that somehow conveyed innocuousness. "I had hoped that my quest was over and I could quickly return home."

"And they fled," he noted, willing to probe the woman mentally. "Not just you, but your authority. Why was that?"

Ramazan was an expert poker player. He didn't use those skills at the table all that often, unless compelled, but he could read most people better than they could themselves.

Whatever she was about to say was going to be an interesting blend of truth and lies, mixed together well enough that nobody would probably be able to separate them later.

He smiled at her as she leaned forward and drew a breath.

"Dave Hall was formerly a member of the Dominion Household," she said quietly. "I won't demand that such information never leave this office, because I'm not a fool. Sheriff. He betrayed me and killed the Dominator. The government sent me after him because hell itself won't be far enough for that man to escape me."

Ramazan nodded. He had suspected Tarasicodissa and Hall had bigger problems than they had let on, especially from the way Valentinian and his first mate had danced obliquely around the subject before, telling him he was better off not knowing the truth, lest more assassins come.

Briefly, Ramazan wondered if he would have to face such trouble, over and above the hard men and women that occasionally called on his station.

"Killed the Dominator?" Ramazan confirmed, letting some level of wonder into his voice anyway, just to see what she said. "He's the assassin?"

"He is," she growled in a quiet, angry voice. "I imagine that makes him a national hero in Laurentia, except that the old Dominator knew better than to attack you, and the new one might not learn those lessons for a while."

Ramazan nodded in turn. Laurentia was one of the Dominion's closest neighbors, and relations had been hot and cold over the centuries. The new Dominator might take a dim view of Bohrne Station hosting their prey, however briefly and innocently.

However, Ramazan was reasonably sure that Valentinian wasn't coming back to this side of Wildspace for a few decades, if ever. Precisely because of this woman seated across from him. And what she represented

Hell indeed hath no fury.

"They're gone," Ramazan said after a moment of political contemplation.

He liked the kid. Respected that Valentinian was truly trying to do the right thing with a bad hand, rather than just folding his cards and pulling up stakes. Hopefully, they had already run far enough to put this woman off their trail.

Or could outrun her some more.

He didn't want this praying mantis on his deck, either. Not one second longer than he had to have her.

Still, there was money to be made.

Besides that, Stephaneria was still supremely pissed at Tarasicodissa for just abandoning her here, despite what his niece had called several near seductions. He'd even seen one of them.

Ramazan couldn't find it in himself to blame the lad. Three women, all smart and attractive, any one of whom would have been more than amenable to a tumble.

If he wanted to alienate the other two.

In the end, Valentinian had probably done the only thing he could and hired himself a professional companion for the evening.

But Stephaneria took it hard. Forty-four, divorced, and competing with women much younger for the attentions of eligible men.

"They are gone, yes," the woman said. "But someone on this station might know where they went."

"I might have a few ideas, myself," Ramazan said. "And know a few others with clues. Why should we help?"

That broke through her shell. Like perhaps she had been considering her own suggestion of a tumble and suddenly had a reason to make it business as well. She leaned forward in such a way that a simple blouse probably would have shown off an ample amount of cleavage, were she not engulfed in those robes.

Still, he had seen her before, dressed less formally. He could imagine.

"How far have they run?" she guessed fairly accurately, a slight grin settling on her features.

"Deep into Wildspace," Ramazan grinned back.

"And they'll never pass back through this sector, will they?"

"That was my understanding, last time I spoke with the group of them," Ramazan obliged. "Didn't get all the answers I was looking for. You've given me some of them."

"Dave Hall was my husband, Sheriff," she said simply, letting some of her ice melt to show the woman underneath. "His betrayal becomes mine by extension. I can never go back to the Dominion either. Not really. They might pension me off and forget about me within a month if I'm lucky. I'll never have what I did before."

Ramazan let his eyes roam over her face, her concealed figure, his mind filling in the details from before. Truly a physically impressive woman. Perhaps a touch too much cruelty in the face and hands, but this woman was never a simpering innocent.

Her air changed as she watched him watching her. The hard edges were still there, but she did something to soften them. Made herself less of a statue and more of a woman.

"There are other things I might seek," she said after a second. "Personal things entirely separate from matters of state. My husband and I had grown aloof from one another, and no other man would dare approach me. Even today."

"Separate from matters of state?" Ramazan asked in a light tone, listening to the sudden huskiness in her voice.

"Bribes are just for information," she replied with a hint of a smile. "We might talk of other things as well."

She leaned forward again, seducing him with only her eyes.

"After all, I'll depart here once I have the trail, and probably never return," she offered, one hand suddenly resting in the middle of his desk, palm up.

He knew that for what it was. This woman was trapped in that same celibacy that the Sheriff of Bohrne Station fell into. In his case, it was easier to just watch and not involve himself with any of the lovely women that lived here. If he occasionally engaged with strangers passing through, those were his off-hours.

The Ambassador would never have off-hours if she was part of the Dominion's inner workings. But one niggling thought crept into the back of his head as he held out a hand and she took it.

Her skin was warm.

The only reason Ramazan could think of that no man would dare touch a woman like her was if her husband was somebody other than a mere soldier like Dave Hall. He might need to be the Dominator himself to command that sort of deadly power. And she had said *Matters of State*. That suggested Hall had been high in the government himself.

But she had not been lying about the man. The rage in her eyes was that of a wife betrayed.

He just hoped those boys had gotten a good, running start, because he wasn't about to keep this woman around here any longer than necessary.

The only way all this made any sense was if Dave Hall had actually been the Dominator himself. That thought was insane, but it was the one thing that explained all those little details he had picked up along the way from all the players involved.

Ramazan rose from his chair and somehow found this woman pressed hungrily up against him as he moved halfway around his desk. He kissed the woman, knowing that he could carve out a few hours of pleasure for himself, and that she would never come back.

Ramazan didn't like trouble on his deck.

PARADISE. Pure and simple. The kind of heat that had been missing in Bayjy's life for so long she had almost forgotten what it tasted like, until they had stepped out of the ship into the noonday sun.

Captain had probably done that especially for her. They could have waited until closer to nightfall to hike over to the city, but the sun had been at meridian when they started and just getting to the hottest, nastiest part of the day as they hit the city limits.

Gods, it felt good to be home. Or home-ish.

Even in a place that was a shithole like this one.

Butler had only occasionally taken his ship and crew to planetary surfaces, so she'd spent the last couple of years on stations or in wrecks, dealing with those frigid temperatures the wimpy humans considered acceptable.

Even the inside of the bar had been a little too cool for her, but she'd gotten a really good warm going, just walking. Like a lizard on a sun-facing rock, she could hold all that absorbed heat for a while, and she had extra clothes in her bag for later, when the sun went down. Wouldn't show off her fantastic bottom as well, but would keep her warm enough, since she'd left her heatsuit back on the ship.

Except Captain and Big Guy had only wanted to stay in that first place long enough to get the lay of the land and some food. Now they were headed to the afternoon sooq that emerged once the temperature got back below forty degrees outside.

Bayjy pulled a sweater out of her bag and slipped it on, wondering if Captain recognized it from his closet. Kyriaki had stolen it for her at some point, some sort of strange game, like sisters borrowing clothes from a brother and never returning them.

Except Kyrie didn't look at Captain like a sibling. Bayjy didn't either, but she was willing to let the blond chick work herself up to dragging the man into a supply closet at some point before Bayjy did.

Or not.

Bayjy was always afraid of hurting a regular human if she got carried away with her orgasms, but Captain was tougher than he let on, and Big Guy was stronger than she was. Not exactly Bayjy's type, but always useful to have a fallback if she got desperate.

Captain and Big Guy were in heads-on-swivels mode right now, silently challenging anything that moved with the threat of explicit, lethal violence. She appreciated the way that a bubble of space quietly moved everywhere with them as a result. And she had money in her pocket, regular pay since Captain had fleeced a couple of big poker games back in Laurentia and could pay her. Plus her share from the cargo they'd hauled to Begzatlari.

Speaking of which…

Bayjy located a table with various fresh and dried fruits. And the fact that the people buying looked like locals. Not that there were any tourists on this planet, but spacers had a different look about them. More like Captain.

She tapped Valentinian on the arm and led him to the stall. Perusing, she bought a bag of dried dates and a second bag of dried figs. These were a breed she didn't know. Dried, they were still almost the size of fresh apricots.

And she was still technically a fixer, having found Captain that cargo of fresh fruit the last time.

"Are you the middleman or the farmer?" Bayjy queried the old, dried husk of a man behind the table.

She nibbled on a date. It tasted like brown honey in her hands. Wow.

The dealer eyeballed her, noting the sweatshirt pulled a little tight across her chest. And her skin. She felt mauve today.

"Middleman," he finally said in that odd accent the locals all seemed to have, each syllable almost its own word. "Why?"

"Last cargo I found us was coconuts and pineapples," she said. "Almost out of leftover stock we kept for personal use. Plus I want more fruit as well. We don't have a hydroponics station on the ship anymore."

Bayjy had heard Valentinian's explanation of what a black thumb he had. And she knew the man wasn't about to give up his armory and the *freaking enormous* collection of weapons he had somehow accumulated. Most crews needed about a dozen guns total. Captain had something closer to two hundred in there. Every size, shape, and flavor she had ever imagined. Plus a few.

"Wrong season," the merchant said after a moment. "Both temperate zones grow food crops, alternating on seasons. Local produce is from greenhouses."

"Dried is fine," Bayjy said, noting how Captain and Big Guy were lurking close, protecting her flanks and letting her talk. "Looking for ten or twenty kilograms total weight for the ship, not for a transport cargo."

Butler had never let anyone else speak for him, convinced that the shorter species were all too stupid to tie their own shoes without his supervision. But Butler had been born an asshole.

"Come back two days," the man said, holding up fingers. "I talk other dealers and we assemble trunk for you. Same pound price, since box included."

Bayjy noted the price she'd paid for the two bags she had tucked into her pouch and nodded to the man. They could haggle from there, but that wasn't all that bad a price to begin with.

She smiled at Captain and let him lead for now. He took them towards a part of the sooq where the spaces were more permanent, small shops off of a covered arcade done in a local stone about the color of aged honey. One of them sold incense, probably a gold mine on a planet where nobody bathed and sonic showers were apparently viewed as the Devil's medicine.

She'd known a few people like that. They always had a stick of incense burning.

Second one was a tea shop. Or maybe coffee. Mix

of both, in two-, five-, and twenty-kilo bags of each. Raw prices weren't incredibly stupid, but she didn't have the equipment to roast her own beans back on the ship. And wasn't sure Captain would ever allow that inside his life support system.

Third bay seemed to be the place Captain was after. He ducked in first, with Bayjy on his cute butt. Big Guy stationed himself at the door like a male caryatid statue with a big gun.

Huh. Books. Lots of them. All bound in leather, from the looks of it, rather than cloth. Probably easier, since a lot of the local economy involved raising critters. Cotton would have to come up from the coast, or down from the temperate zones.

The kitchen, upstairs on *Longshot*, was bigger than this store, but the owner had made the place a compact maze you entered by passing him in a little cubby, before heading deeper, questing for the minotaur.

Captain stopped suddenly and she plowed into him, eyes elsewhere.

"Sorry," she said, setting him back on the ground after her first instinct had been to pick up the slightly-shorter and lighter man so she didn't bounce him into a bookshelf.

The look she got back was sarcasm so distilled it brought a smile to her face. Another smile. More smiley, or something.

"Yes?" the proprietor perked up.

Human, Bayjy decided, looking at him. Just old and leathery. Sharp eyes, though.

"I collect old maps," Captain said, kinda sideways. "And ancient histories, going back to the wars."

She liked the way he didn't ask any questions or anything. And it was pretty much honest truth.

"You read Urlan?" he asked.

"Some," Captain said.

"Yes," Bayjy butted in. "Fluently."

"Right-hand corner," the proprietor looked up at her and nodded knowingly. "Blue spine row and below. Then we talk maps."

Captain led and she made sure not to run him over this time.

"Fluent?" he murmured as they got there.

"Salvaging is a multi-lingual game, Captain," she whispered back. "Lots of money on Urlan paraphernalia, if you can avoid the junk."

"Like?" he asked, a little surprised.

"Like this one," Bayjy reached out and touched a spine with a purple finger. "Unless you're into Urlan love poetry, that is. Not judging."

He laughed quietly.

"We'll save that for a rainy day."

"Ain't no rainy days on…Right. Gotcha," she smiled back. "What are you looking for?"

"War ended two thousand years ago," Captain said. "Planetary geography probably hasn't changed much, but I figure any history of this planet in Urlan is going to deal with the wars and include maps. I need identifiable locations I can triangulate to in the modern age, and everything is going to be relative, rather than fixed."

"Huh," Bayjy grunted.

Made sense. Dude was sharp. She did a quick scan of titles, pulling one down and rifling through it quickly enough.

"Maybe," she offered weakly. "Like, fourth choice behind asking random strangers in the street?"

"Understood." Captain nodded. "You keep looking here and I'll try a different tack."

She heard him approach the dealer again as she read.

"How about the conquest of Kryuome after the wars?" he asked. "Older the better."

Bayjy glanced over in time to see a bill slide across the counter and vanish into a gnarled hand. Old guy got a sly look in that maze of canyons on his face.

The man stood up and pulled a book from the shelf behind him, placing it flat on the counter and opening it. Bayjy slid her current tome carefully back and meandered that direction. Captain was turning pages like he was holding a holy relic when she got there.

She couldn't tell what he saw, but she heard his breath change pitch. Captain looked up with a hard, shrewd look in his eyes.

"Yes," he said simply. "How much?"

"One thousand Union Krodageni," the merchant beamed back.

Bayjy nearly swallowed her tongue. That was a lot of money.

"Four hundred," Captain laughed and fired back. "And that other book as well. Maybe I'll go higher if you've got some nice wall maps I can hang in the dining area for entertainment."

She'd watched the man play poker. Lost a reasonable amount of cash to him and the Sheriff in that long con, but she didn't hold that against him. He'd bought her dinner and hired her later on. Plus rescued her from ever having to go planetside to pick fruit for a living.

The old man was just as sharp, though. Numbers flowed back and forth like a ball being volleyed by professional athletes. Insults were traded, as well as compliments. The old man brought out a set of maps, ink on hide, and they argued about those for a while, too.

Bayjy went back and looked at more books, settling on something that looked like a colonization report that had been misfiled as a romance. She hoped it had been misfiled, since the strange breeds of Variant Humanity called Muties had been living here when the explorer who wrote the book arrived.

She returned to the front with the book and set it on the counter, next to the first book and a map. That set off a whole other round of dickering and haranguing.

About the time she was going to go look for some hot coffee to tide her over, the two duelers came to an agreement. Hands were shook. The old man even smiled.

"Six hundred, thirty-eight Union Krodageni, plus you come back with the story, when you find whatever it is you seeking, young man," the proprietor beamed. "I have not had so much fun selling a book in more than a decade."

"If we can," Captain more or less shaded the promise as she listened. Lord only knew what would happen out there. "If we can."

"Indeed," the old man nodded. "Seek out Basuk for armaments. He is cousin and I send good word, although he will not believe me that you know how to properly negotiate, so I suggest you pee ahead of time and prepare for a long fight."

The smile on the man's face was almost as good as Bayjy'd had all day, so they shared it as Valentinian counted out bills and the old man sold them a cloth bag like her messenger to carry things in. Cute and semi-antique, too, with brass fittings and reinforced corners. Probably rain-proof, but they'd have to keep it and find a planet where water fell out of the sky to check. Scorpion-proof, maybe?

Still, a good deal done, from the smiles everyone shared.

They emerged from the shop and Bayjy noted the sun was just about to the horizon in the west.

"Now what?" she aked.

"Home," Captain said.

She took the lead, just because it was starting to cool off and the walk would keep her warm. Valentinian was behind her, with Dave in the rear. The way was rough, climbing some hills and through a few wadis to get to where Kyrie and the ship had been left.

They were about halfway there when a man stepped out from behind a small cliff with a pistol in one hand and smiled at them.

[7]

KYRIAKI

AFTER SO LONG WITH the four of them aboard the ship, Kyriaki was happy to have the place to herself for a while. She'd never really been a people person, Bayjy notwithstanding, and the thought of spending an afternoon in a mob sounded about as exciting as shaving her legs with a table saw.

At least Valentinian had relaxed some around her. There were still sparks, occasionally, but they were mostly the hungry-for-touch kind and not the punch-you-in-the-face sort. And he had finally let her into the armory room.

Dominion Prime, the Dominator's Winter Palace orbiting Cronus Prime, might have more guns than *Longshot Hypothesis*, but it would be a close go. She hadn't asked why the man kept enough firepower to start a small war. Kyriaki wasn't a cop anymore.

Probably never be a cop again, unless they really did somehow end up on the far side of Wildspace with new identities. She could see getting herself a gig like that Sheriff had, back at Bohrne, when she reached that age. That was the sort of thing that suited her temperament.

After that, there was really nothing to do. Daily chores and maintenance never slacked, but nowadays that just meant that everyone pitched in and it took about an hour to complete. She wasn't much of a reader, either, in spite of the amazingly diverse library Valentinian had collected in the ship's data core.

In the end, she decided she did want some sun. Not much. Just enough to maybe have some tan that was natural, and not a result of standing in the booth in the bathroom for your regular dose of Vitamin D.

She was alone. *Longshot Hypothesis* was locked up tight and sitting atop a small plateau north of the city a couple of kilometers away, so she could look down and see it. Valentinian had turned on both sets of alarms, so she felt safe enough.

Kyriaki found herself up on the top of the ship, through the dorsal hatch, between the engines and almost directly over the bridge. One quick look around confirmed that nobody was above her, unless they were flying, and she'd hear them, so she dropped back down into the cooler air and packed.

Big bottle of water. Suntan lotion. Some dried meat and fruit. Small pistol. Big, freaking rifle. Long robes. Towel.

Back up in the sun, she spread the towel on the deck, lotioned herself up, and stretched out naked to get some tan. She had no lines now, so she'd just end up more tan, if anybody noticed, which she doubted.

Turning over after a while, she could see the city below, peeking over the hull like a chipmunk.

The men she saw approaching probably thought

they were being sneaky. They were, if you were looking out from the bridge window, nearly down at ground level, rather than her perch clear up in the sky.

Six of them. Armed, like everyone on this planet, although maybe a little heavier, since two of them had weapons larger than pistols on shoulder straps. They didn't do a half-bad job of setting up an ambush, either, and she was an expert on that topic.

For a moment, she wondered what the laws would say if she just opened fire on them from up here when the time came. Valentinian had suggested that there was no planetary government at all, and barely even regional authority. This could be one of those places where might actually made right.

There was even the perfect hunting rifle resting next to her on the upper hull. Long-barreled slugthrower firing caseless ammunition, it was designed to bring down massive predators at long range. She suspected that it would also do a nasty number on a lightly-armored police flyer on most planets.

Valentinian wasn't the sort to collect trophy heads of critters in a den while smoking a pipe.

Tempting. Two moons would be overhead tonight, so she would have enough light. And there was most certainly a nightscope in there somewhere that she could attach, if she wanted to.

Watching them, all six took up positions on the trail to catch Valentinian and the others by surprise. The trail kinked in such a way that you'd be right in the ambush before anybody moved.

Kyriaki saw red. She couldn't place her finger on

what it was, but the rage swelling out of her belly was nasty.

She slid back carefully out of sight and grabbed all her gear, not bothering to put the robe on, but merely carrying it with the rest. Down the hatch and into the kitchen, she left most of her gear there, and went to get dressed.

The old bodysuit in burgundy was back in storage on Dominion Prime. Or the Widow had burned all of her leftover gear on *Dominion-427*. All she had now was civilian attire: brown pants that tucked into her boots; blue T-shirt with a cartoon character on the front; green kepi in place of her white beret that had been a symbol of her authority as the Dominion's Security Bureau.

The White Hats.

She added a holster for her pistol and grabbed a short-range plasma rifle. Never know when you might want prisoners, and she doubted that the city had a good-enough clinic to treat flamer blasts to the chest, especially if your buddies had to carry you a couple of kilometers to get there.

Kyriaki tied her hair back and added a shock rod to her belt at the last minute. She let herself out the rear airlock, away from the ambush. There was a code key programmed into her card reader. That and a password were both needed to open the ship back up, so nobody would get in while she was out. If they tried, the alarm sirens might be audible from the city.

Time to sneak.

This was what she missed, as she slid to her right and followed a small wadi that would bring her around behind the men poised and waiting for her friends. The sun was getting low in the sky, so she knew they would be headed this direction soon.

Valentinian would have sent a message if they were held up or staying overnight, just so she didn't feel the need to bring up the heavy support firepower and rescue them.

Like now.

Longshot Hypothesis held the high ground, so her path was generally downhill. Stalking her prey like the old days, when she was a cop and they were rebels or criminals. Threats to her lord, The Dominator. Which almost made her giggle, when she remembered that Dave Hall had been the Dominator she had sworn to serve, in their previous lifetimes.

Now he was her friend. It was weird having friends, but she would protect them.

Kyriaki had memorized the terrain from above. Four of the men were on the right as she approached, ready to fire down from the hilltop if they had to, while the other two were below, where they would no doubt confront Valentinian with guns and bluster, and probably surprise.

The terrain around here was scrub desert. Rocks and dried dirt for the most part, with weird tumbleweeds and cactus-like plants on the slope. Not thick, but enough to provide her some level of cover if she moved carefully, especially with the sun low behind her.

And silence, covered over anyways with a slight wind from the south. They wouldn't be able to smell her, either, if they had been moose.

The man in charge had set up his trap in a way so dumb Kyriaki wondered if they had seen her and set up a double trap. She froze and looked all directions, but nothing moved except a snake suddenly backing away from her with a beetle stuck in its mouth.

Kyriaki had never seen a snake slither backwards.

She could see the backs of two heads, and two more were down and around the shoulder of the hill. They were so far apart that she could take each one individually. At the same time, she couldn't just shoot them all from here, like she could have from her perch atop the ship.

Personal felt better, though.

Forward, she slung the plasma rifle and drew her pistol and the shock rod. The closest man was poised over a rifle of some sort, head low on the crest of the hill and motionless in a way that suggested Valentinian was already approaching.

Kyriaki pointed her pistol at the second man, around ten meters to her right, but he would have to sit up and turn around to see her here. Good enough.

Rage.

The cop in her grounded the shock rod into the man's thigh and held it there while he twitched like a gigged frog. The only sound was a brief gurgle as he passed out, and the other man didn't hear it. She was a good-enough shot to take the second man with her off-hand, had she needed to.

Freeze. Look. Listen. Number two didn't move.

Kyriaki crept forward, staying below the crest. Number two thrashed a little when she nailed him with the shock rod, but again very little noise. And the breeze was blowing away from everyone to hear it or smell her.

She paused enough to look over the hill both ways. Two more men had taken up spots in the brush, one behind a cactus and the other in a slight dip that might hold water for a few days when the rainy season did pass through here.

The other two men were down in the defile, watching the trail where Bayjy was leading the other two uphill. All considered, Bayjy wasn't paranoid enough for this kind of place. Valentinian or Dave would have been in better position, or at least not as exposed. She'd need to take the salvager aside at some point and give the woman some lessons on hunting men.

And she was out of time. Bayjy was just about to the critical point, and there was no time for Kyriaki to slip back down the slope out of sight of the two men on her flank. Another ten minutes and she could have done it.

Kyriaki kept the profanities on the inside. She slipped the shock rod into her belt and reached behind her for the plasma rifle.

More than one way to skin a moose.

[8]
VALENTINIAN

VALENTINIAN SAW the ambush as soon as the man stepped out. He almost managed to say something, but the man stepping into view had a pistol on them already and a second person appeared a moment later.

Valentinian quick-scanned to his left and saw the other heads indicating that he and Dave had stepped right into a pile of fresh gator poop.

Human. Or a close enough Variant in the lesser light of sunset. Dressed like a spacer, too, except some of the gear was local, so maybe someone who had lost his ship or his ride at some point and gotten stranded here.

Valentinian grimaced at his stupidity in walking into a trap. Hopefully, these men just wanted to rob them. He didn't have that much money on him, nor weapons, but he did have Dave behind him, hopefully thinking evil and dangerous thoughts.

Everyone came to a halt. Valentinian knew trying to draw right now would get him shot, but they hadn't fired, either, so maybe talking was on the menu, instead.

"Captain," the big man over there said in a growly kind of voice.

"That's right," Valentinian replied. "If you'd wanted to talk, we were only going up to the ship for the night. Tomorrow, need to make some inquiries about supplies and maybe hiring some locals for a few tasks."

It even sounded reasonable. What he needed right now was enough of a distraction that he and Dave could do something. Hopefully Bayjy would be smart enough to drop immediately if all hell broke loose.

The man started to say something, when a pair of dull whumps suddenly rose above them in the still air, like a giant stomping both feet in the dirt.

Valentinian looked to his left, surprised when he was still standing. That had sounded an awful lot like a plasma rifle, cycling two shots.

He smiled when Kyriaki suddenly stood up from the top of the hill and pointed the smoking, glowing barrel at the men in the defile with him. It looked like an onrushing supernova in the gathering dusk. Like one of the moons had exploded somehow and you could only watch it silently.

"Drop your weapons before I kill you," she yelled angrily. "Your four friends are already down."

The two bandits had made the classic mistake of turning towards Kyriaki's voice. By the time they glanced back, Valentinian and Dave had guns pointed at them.

As did Bayjy, which was pretty impressive.

"Last warning," Kyriaki yelled.

"Talk or die," Valentinian said in a hard voice as the two men suddenly were out-numbered, out-gunned, and probably out of luck.

"Talk?" the man said.

"Drop the gun," Kyriaki sounded like a Death Angel up there.

Both pistols hit the dirt at the same time. Happily, neither of them went off when they did.

Bayjy surprised him by circling to the left, out of his and Dave's line of fire. She holstered her weapon, stayed in a squat as she grabbed both of theirs, and glanced back over her shoulder at where Kyriaki had everyone covered.

Valentinian laughed out loud when Bayjy suddenly exploded outward and punched the second man in the groin so hard he folded up around her fist with a screaming whoosh of air and pain.

She stood up right next to the leader and looked down on him with a growl loud enough for Valentinian to hear. The man turned white. Whiter, anyway, from his tan.

"Sit down before I hurt you," Bayjy snarled.

Valentinian had never heard or seen this side of his salvager. Kinda impressive, but she probably had to deal with a lot of crap back on *Hard Bargain* with that M'Rai captain. And whoever else bothered her. She might be cute and female, but she was still big and strong.

And extremely girlie, from the times she had left her laundry in the dryer overnight.

The bandit dropped like a sack of potatoes.

"Dave?" Kyriaki yelled. "A little help up here? Bayjy, you too. Valentinian can handle those two."

He laughed out loud. The last few years, he had

been the muscle of the organization, because Artaxerxes was a middle-aged, squishy engineer.

It might be kinda fun, being the brains for a while.

Valentinian kept his pistol centered on the man from about five meters away as he found a nice rock to rest his butt on. The other dude finally managed to crawl to one side and sit upright, but he had apparently suffered a concussion at some point. Maybe face-planting on the ground when he got punched.

Dave had one man over each shoulder when he returned, and each of the women carried one as well. Seriously, it was nice being around women capable of kicking everybody's ass if they had to.

Four bodies got piled up next to the fifth. Two were smoking from plasma shots, but everyone was moving by now. Bayjy made a point of collecting everyone's boots and tying the laces together so she could carry them. The rock around here would still burn your feet for a few hours.

"So, why should I not have my bloodthirsty crew finish you off?" Valentinian asked with a wolfish grin. "Pretty sure the vultures would appreciate fresh meat, and nobody down there would probably miss you."

[9]
DAVE

If cats had nine lives. Dave figured he might have just used up number three. Or four, depending on a couple of other situations that could have gone either way.

They'd gotten slack. Lazy. He had fallen off that fine, killing edge that the Dominator had been required to maintain at all times. Something about retiring and living the life of the average criminal. He needed to ramp things up, just a bit.

Although, looking at Kyriaki's victims, maybe not. She'd done an exceptional job of taking out four men without them even realizing she was there, Dave wondered if there might have been six bodies tied up and waiting when they got here, if they'd taken another ten or fifteen minutes in town.

"So, why should I not have my bloodthirsty crew finish you off?" Vee asked the punk in charge. "Pretty sure the vultures would appreciate fresh meat, and nobody down there would probably miss you."

Dave enjoyed the look of appalled shock that

remained on the man's face. Clearly, just another bully boy with some friends, used to dealing with average spacers who weren't prepared to unleash unmitigated violence at the drop of a hat. Never had to face someone like him. Or Kyriaki.

"Boss wants to talk to you," the man gurgled, still trying to find his voice.

"He could have sent *one* of you," Vee snarled. "Knocked politely on the hatch. Or maybe walked up to say hello while we were having dinner. Now I'm kinda angry. And you haven't answered my question."

Dave could imagine what an angry Valentinian might be like. Those were the sorts of reasons he had picked the young man in the first place. Boundless luck, mixed with a long, ugly streak of ruthlessness, according to records that had never proven a criminal act.

"We were supposed to take you to him," the man managed, shock settling into his system.

Probably the heat coming off the barrel of Kyriaki's plasma rifle, pointed at his face.

"With guns out?" Valentinian's laugh sounded like a wolf barking. "I'd ask what kind of fool you take me for, but that much is already obvious."

Dave grinned when Vee turned to Bayjy.

"Bring their boots," he ordered. "They can walk home."

Bayjy nodded. She was a little paler than usual, but her previous exposure to violence had been, as near as he could tell, mostly bar fights and drunk crewmates who didn't necessarily want to take *No* for an answer. At least the first time.

Dave settled for glowering at the men. It wasn't

as effective as Kyriaki, but she'd taken out four of them by herself, so she had an extra edge there. Plus a plasma rifle.

"Tell your boss to send someone else, next time. Someone polite and unarmed," Vee snarled at the man. "I ever see you again, anywhere on this planet, I'm going to open fire and assume it was self-defense. You understand me?"

"Yes, sir," the man flinched.

Bullies were always such fragile creatures, at least when they ran into someone willing to fight back. That was part of what made them bullies.

Dave squatted down and made a point of memorizing faces. He would be willing to shoot any of them right now, had Vee ordered it. He let his face tell them that.

Nobody peed themselves, but it was probably a close thing, especially when Bayjy growled at them after he was done.

Valentinian started walking without a glance back. Dave prodded Bayjy to follow, and then he and Kyriaki mentally flipped a coin and she ended up at the rear of the column for the last two hundred meters to the ship.

They ended up upstairs in the lounge, with Vee pulling some juice out of the fridge and the rest of them doing something similar.

"What's this?" Dave asked as he saw the pile of stuff Kyriaki had apparently left on the counter earlier. He picked up a bottle and sniffed it. Coconut.

"Suntan lotion," she replied quietly, grabbing the bottle out of his hand. "I was sunbathing on the top of the ship when they arrived and set up their ambush."

Dave did a double take at the woman when he realized she had probably been nude at the time. He had seen her naked before. When she first came aboard, they had made her strip everything off, which they then jettisoned into warpspace.

But there was a difference between naked and nude.

She started blushed furiously now.

Interestingly, Vee was blushing as well, so maybe those two had accidentally locked eyes at the wrong moment. Or the right one.

Dave hoped that they would finally get over themselves at some point and make a final decision, either to fool around, or not to. The stress of thinking about it constantly wasn't doing either of them any good.

"Okay," Valentinian announced as they all got settled. "Obviously, we've rattled some cages, just settling down on this planet. I have no idea what, who, or why."

"Will the boss send a smarter messenger next time?" Bayjy asked. "Or are they going to just attack us?"

"Don't know," Vee replied with a shrug. "I do know that Dave and I will take turns on watch tonight, with the short-range sensors turned on to make sure they don't show up. If they do, I'm fine taking off on short notice and going somewhere else. If we had guns, I'm almost angry enough to strafe someone right now. Or set up top with a longrifle and snipe."

"Should I anyway?" Kyriaki asked.

"No, but thank you for saving our asses," Vee smiled at her. "No clue what their boss wants. Not a lot of trade or traffic on this planet to work with, other than the need for guns wherever we go."

"Should we break out the nasty stuff?" Dave asked with a grimace.

"Just how nasty can y'all get?" Bayjy seemed to have gotten pale again.

"Extremely," Kyriaki spoke up. "I had my pick of things to take. Plasma rifle seemed best, on the assumption that we might want to interrogate prisoners. Had a lovely sniper rifle with me earlier, when I was up top nude."

Most blushing. Even Dave felt himself get into the act. Kyriaki as primitive war goddess painted in coconut oil. Bayjy grinned at her friend.

"We still going down to talk to this Basuk fellow?" Bayjy asked Vee.

"Yes, but mostly for some sort of short-range transport," Valentinian said. "Maybe they'll have something else I want to buy, but nobody really appreciates my collection."

"Where did all that come from, anyway?" Kyriaki fixed her bright, blue eyes on the man. "I don't think my White Hat detachment back home had that many guns."

Dave liked the way Vee's eyes lit up at first. He'd heard the story earlier. And known parts of it before he lined the man up to make his own escape.

Valentinian laughed and took a deep drink of his juice.

"Honestly?" he asked after a few moments. "I was in a bar fight and took two guys down with a chair. They both had guns, and I wasn't about to let them come after me later, so I took the pistols away from them. Kept them, because having an unregistered firearm hidden about the ship might be a useful thing from time to time. Especially if I get a boarder sneaking in through the forward airlock and finding me upstairs working on an engine."

"You have guns hidden up there?" Kyriaki's eyes got serious. "In addition to all the rest in the armory?"

Dave smiled. Vee smiled. Kyriaki's mouth dropped open.

"Should I?" Dave asked expectantly.

"Go ahead," Vee said.

Dave moved around the table to one of the legs that attached it to the deck permanently. He found the burr and pulled on it while pushing a different place under the tabletop itself. A lock clicked and the leg opened to reveal a secret compartment. And a hold-out pistol.

"How many…?"

"Every room on this ship," Valentinian said solemnly. "Including your quarters. I'll show you where and how to get to them later. For now, I had a collection started. And more bar fights. I started keeping them, rather than chucking them down drains or out airlocks. A few times I did runs for arms dealers, and started swapping this for that. And bought a few pieces outright. Stole a few. What we do to survive. I won't call it a compulsion, but the galaxy is a dangerous place, and up until very recently, it was me and Artaxerxes against some mean people."

"Kinda nice to have friends?" Bayjy asked.

"You have no idea," Vee smiled at her.

"So what books did you buy?" Dave asked.

"Nearly forgot, but you two were having a grand time in the bookstore."

"I need the local geography, but backwards in time," Valentinian said. "We have an old treasure map, and I want to find the big X on it. Don't really need to deal with the locals all that much, but I'm also not going to take any shit from neighborhood warlord punks. When you're on duty, I'm going to read. If we're lucky, we can talk to Basuk tomorrow and then go deal with the Muties down on the equator."

"And if we're not?" Kyriaki asked.

"Then maybe I burn the whole, damned city down first," Valentinian said with a hard smile. "I'm not playing around."

[10]
ATHANASIA

SHE HAD GOTTEN quarters on the station for herself and installed her bodyguards close by, once Athanasia had returned to duty. Or however it was she wanted to quantify the morning after the lovely evening she had just spent.

Ramazan had fallen asleep wrapped around her, breathing in her ear. She had even fallen asleep herself, which surprised her in ways she had forgotten were possible. Her celibacy had been years in the making.

Several days had passed. She still seemed to have a bounce in her step that suggested she needed to add that sort of thing to her regular calendar. Not aboard the ship, but most stations could service those needs.

Yes, it might even be something to look forward to, besides hunting down Dave Hall and killing him. Not even building a small network of spies on this station had done so much for her humor.

Tonight, she was in a private room at a select club,

awaiting the next step in her revenge. She had dressed formally, back into those white robes that conveyed Dominion authority. Ramazan had arranged for her to meet his niece, another woman with an axe to grind, if the rumor mill was to be believed.

The door was opened by a flunky and the woman arrived. Athanasia rose and took her hand.

Stephaneria was divorced and in her mid-forties, so a decade younger than Athanasia, but she had that same burning rage underneath.

Athanasia had gotten some pieces of the story from Ramazan, but not much. Enough, to lead her to other questions. Other sources of information.

A few other people on the station had even been willing to be bribed for things she didn't know after she knew what to ask.

And what Stephaneria thought about Tarasicodissa.

"Welcome," she said as the younger woman got settled. "Your uncle and I have spoken a few times, and I'd like to bribe you personally for some information, starting with dinner."

She liked the way the other woman's eyes got shrewd and hooded. They could make common ground, but were still technically enemies from radically different worlds: socially, politically, economically.

And Athanasia represented Stephaneria in another decade alone, perhaps. She could use that as an edge, as well.

"You're hunting Dave Hall and Valentinian Tarasicodissa?" the woman asked.

Athanasia caught the hint of emphasis on the

latter name. Yes, there was a place to stick a knife, as her recent contacts on the station had suggested.

"I am," Athanasia nodded. "My mission is to kill Hall, but I also intend to punish the others as well."

Punish, rather than just *Kill*. The woman might still have some emotional attachment to the captain. Many other women apparently had, from what the records had shown, including Inspector Apokapes, for example.

But then, you've been thrown over for one of the two women Valentinian chose to take with him, leaving you behind, didn't he? That's what the rumors all say. And I can see it in your eyes.

"And you believe I can help you?" Stephaneria pressed in a hard, quiet voice.

"Punishing those two women with him goes hand in hand with what I plan to do to the men," Athanasia emphasized. "Without your helping me, they might all escape justice and live out long and happy lives elsewhere."

Leaving you here to be an old maid librarian, stuck in a forgotten corner of the station while others have adventures? Yes, I know your fears.

The needles went under the woman's skin easily. She almost flinched under the words, so closely had Athanasia read her. So well had the watchers known the librarian and her weaknesses.

"Punish?" Stephaneria said almost unconsciously.

"Dave Hall was my husband, before all this started," Athanasia used a longer needle this time. Almost a nail. "He abandoned me. Embarrassed me. *Left me behind.*"

Had she slapped the woman, the flinches may have been about the same. As might the rage that suddenly took root in those eyes. Rumors had mentioned the previous husband and the affairs that had broken the marriage apart. That was another avenue that she could use.

"I want to make that man pay for what he did to me," Athanasia continued in a cold, hard voice.

"Yes," Stephaneria breathed. "I understand that."

"I thought you might," Athanasia let her voice soften.

Two women, letting their hair down to bitch about men. As it were.

She let the moment stretch as the other woman flushed and paled alternately under the twin forces of some internal battle.

"I understand you might know where they've gone," Athanasia stated quietly. "Can you help me?"

Soft. Supple. The two of us against all the men out there. How great is your rage?

"I don't want them to win," Athanasia continued as the woman remained silent, breathing the words more than speaking them, but the impact on the younger woman was an electric shock.

"No," Stephaneria growled suddenly. "He doesn't get to win."

Athanasia didn't ask which *He* that might be. Revenge would be broad and inclusive. She waited and watched the woman's anger boil slowly. They were almost over the rim of the pot now already.

"I might know where they're going," Stephaneria admitted finally.

Ramazan had hinted as much, without understanding how far she might chase those men. Brags about a crooked card game and a treasure map had never been confirmed, but she wasn't looking for evidence to put before a magistrate. Just a direction she could sail, on her way to the gates of hell.

"Tell me," Athanasia conspired with her, both of their voices low but picking up energy.

"There is a map," Stephaneria said.

Athanasia fought to keep the glee out of her eyes as she nodded conspiratorially, watching this woman twist herself in her jealous rage at being *left behind*.

"A treasure map," the woman continued. "Tarasicodissa had it, but couldn't tell where it was in the galaxy, so he asked me to help. Bribed me, even."

"I'd like to bribe you," Athanasia offered in a husky voice that was entirely ambiguous about *how*.

Stephaneria's eyes flashed hot under the emotional assault inside her soul. Her smile was a dark, almost malevolent thing that Athanasia recognized from her mirror.

"I found it for him," she said, but her eyes had lost focus now, deep inside where the maelstrom of fire and wind fought. "But he left me here. Took *them* with him. Seduced me with his eyes and his words, and then abandoned me."

Yes. I have you now. Tell me, little one. Give me your soul.

"Go on?"

"I know which system," Stephaneria said. "But not where. There were a set of directions and coordinates on one side of the page. He covered those before I copied it. But I have the star and the planet."

"What would convince you to share it with me?" Athanasia asked quietly.

Somehow, they had both ended up leaning

forward, until they were breathing on each other at this point. She took a risk and leaned into the younger woman, brushing lips with her. It seemed to be what Stephaneria needed to boil over the pot entirely.

Her eyes flew open wide and focused on Athanasia, but she didn't withdraw. Flushed instead. Crimsoned to the tips of her ears.

But then her eyes turned utterly feral. Angry. Raging.

She leaned forward herself and returned the kiss. Hot and heavy with emotion.

Athanasia enjoyed the physicality of the woman as she smelled the musk of Stephaneria's hatred start to mix with her own.

The woman finally broke and leaned back. Athanasia did as well, but smiled. Ramazan had been fun, but his niece promised to be even better.

"I want to go with you," the younger woman announced, surprising both of them, it seemed. "I want to see you punish them. Help you. Revel in it for what I owe that man."

"Are you sure?" Athanasia pressed.

Having an second killer that they didn't associate with her would be a wolf in sheep's clothing, especially if the woman was that desperate for human touch.

Athanasia could imagine having weeks or months to twist the woman's hatred, hone it into a sword. It would keep her warm.

"They don't get to win," Stephaneria growled.

Athanasia leaned forward again. The sudden kiss was as hungry as it was angry.

Yes. You'll serve my vengeance nicely.

[11]

GLAXU

GLAXU HAD DECIDED to make his approach during the day. Humans were generally a daytime species, so just showing up on someone's doorstep in the middle of the night was frequently met with weapons and attitude problems.

Outermost was up at a very high altitude this morning, listening on all channels, but he had already locked down his target. Someone was sitting on the ground with an active sensor array pinging every second and a half. Either they were lost and listening for help, or had about the same opinion of the natives that he had.

One way to find out.

He configured the fightercraft's variable geometry for a soft glide and stayed at ten thousand meters elevation. All four wings were out to their widest stretch, and he could almost stall in mid-air this way.

Below, his target was separated from the city by a reasonable walk, which would make for excellent security. He was coming up on it from what he guessed was aft, and was struck by the overall form.

Spacecraft didn't really have to follow any rules of streamlining, since most of the time they didn't have anything more dense than a solar wind to deal with. *Outermost* was designed for atmospheric operations as well, so the central spearhead had two canards and two wings, all multiply-hinged for whatever maneuvering needs you had.

The ship below was a cargo transport, big and somewhat blocky. Interestingly, from here it looked like a Mondi lying flat on the ground, with his legs together and his short wings up and over his head. A rather elegant waste of space, all things considered, but pretty.

The leg section was probably larder and systems. On his scanners, the wings forward were actually engines, so the ship would fly like he did. Or fly where he had to settle for a glide when jumping from a height.

Still, a technological species. That was a step up from the weirdoes further north on the equator. Hopefully they'd be able to help him repair his warp systems so he could get off this rock.

The morning light was just cresting and illuminating the valley where the city hunched angrily. On his screens, he picked up movement. Four humans emerged from the ship that was his target and began to walk.

Glaxu dialed in the magnification as the ship coasted. The humans were heavily armed, even for this planet, so they understood how dangerous the natives were. That boded well. He decided to set down secretly and follow them on foot.

If they weren't from around here, they might not be such assholes.

He let his eyes grin as he flipped *Outermost* over on one wing, pulled in all the lifting surfaces, and pushed the engines over hard.

HE LOOKED up when he detected movement out of the corner of his eyes, tracking something too far away for Valentinian to identify what it was. Aircraft of some sort, moving at a high rate of speed, but away from him, so not currently a threat.

"Dave," he called out anyway.

"Got him," the big man said solemnly.

Valentinian heard the rifle come down from Dave's shoulder. Chamber got checked for a round. Glancing back, Dave was carrying it across his chest now, barrel already pointed in the general direction, just in case.

Valentinian had settled for a heavy flamer pistol this morning. The biggest, ugliest thing he could stuff into a thigh holster. Everyone else had made do with smaller flamers or shock pistols, depending on their mood, but they all had extra guns. Valentinian had an extra shock pistol openly holstered to the side of his boot.

Dave had the sniper rifle. It also just happened to

be a portable rocket launcher, firing a missile the size of the man's thumb. Caseless, so it would just be getting up to a nice speed when it cleared the barrel, en route to hitting ten times the speed of sound on this planet if it traveled three kilometers downrange without hitting anything. Might not bring down a spaceship, but it would certainly thump the hell out of one, and might punch a hole in your shell big enough to let a lot of air out.

Dave had just grinned when Valentinian asked if he could use it effectively. Yeah, former leader of the Caelon Assault troopers knew weapons.

Bayjy was holding one of the plasma rifles today. That would let her intimidate the hell out of people, without sparking a mass casualty incident if she had to open fire. Just lots of bruising and second degree burns. She seemed okay with that outcome. Still pissed about getting ambushed yesterday, but learning to shoot in combat wasn't an overnight task.

Kyriaki had apparently spent more than a little time touring the armory yesterday. She had emerged this time with an assault pulsar that had been hidden clear at the back, a short-range, high-rate-of-cycle version of the pulse carbine or pulse rifles in the closer racks.

Extremely effective at less than fifty yards, and Kyriaki had that same look in her eyes that Bayjy did. Death would be jealous of those two.

Seriously? He could get accustomed to being the wimp in this group, rather than the muscle.

They circled wide around the site of yesterday's fun, along the path Kyriaki had used to sneak up on those city boys. Took a little longer to get down to the flats at the edge of town, but less risk.

They'd find a different way back later.

This town was on its own clock. Locals were setting up the morning sooq when the group passed through. Valentinian checked, but nothing interesting stood out today. He wasn't sure what he wanted, or he'd have mentioned it to someone yesterday. They'd probably find it during the mid-day nap and then have it for sale later if he did.

Other people were just now staggering out of their all-night entertainment, stumbling towards whatever niche or grotto they slept in, away from the heat. Those people were no significant threat this morning.

A few looked at Valentinian and his small army of destruction, but nobody was drunk enough to pick a fight this morning and get their asses kicked. Wasn't something he would expect to hold true every day, but today was good enough.

The bibliophile had given them directions to a compound on the far side of town. Valentinian had considered skirting all the way around, but decided that looked a little too feeble, so he marched them right down the main road in from the south, through the central market and the sooq, and out the other side. Mostly just merchants and a few locals this morning, rather than any of the more dangerous people who apparently fed on travelers and tourists.

Let them. Valentinian was feeling a mite indigestible this morning.

Basuk's compound was obvious, once they cleared the last ring of buildings clustered in tight against each other. If this town had torn down a wall around the outside and built a circling road, Basuk had built just on the outside of that.

Low, stone walls looked just about right for someone to stand behind and fire out, in the event of a mob. All five points of the pentagram had elevated platforms as well. Tiny lighthouses, perhaps, but also sheltered places for a gunman. The metal gate split down the middle and had a patina of rust on it, but Valentinian suspected that it was painted on later, as one of them was open enough to walk in, and they were as thick as his fist. If that was steel, it would weigh tons.

A human with a lightweight rifle waited at the open gate, observing them with a blank face as they approached.

"I was instructed to seek out Basuk," Valentinian said when he was close enough to talk instead of yell. "His cousin sent me."

"You are the book collector," the man said with a sudden smile. "Welcome."

Sure. Why not? If that was the way they wanted to identify him, he could live with it.

Inside, there was a courtyard filled with vehicles. He guessed that's what they were, anyway.

Start with repulsorlifts and a generator. Build just enough frame to count, and then cover most of it with a steel mesh about two centimeters thick. Seat for a driver up front in the center, with a semi-solid slab of metal as a wind blocker, assuming you wore goggles. Turret right behind that, where someone standing could rotate a ring-mounted heavy weapon to engage pedestrians and low-altitude aircraft.

Twenty-five centimeter-high gunwales on the sides would offer minimal protection to people sitting on benches down the middle, facing outward. Or give you a place to rest a barrel when shooting.

Cargo could be stashed in any number of places inside by flipping the benches up, and there were hooks and shelves on the outside of the vehicle as well.

Valentinian checked, and there was a bank of lights across the bow, so you could drive at night. Not fast, but not blind either.

No protection from the sun, whatsoever, so Bayjy would be in heaven and the rest of them would have to wear robes and hats at all times.

He decided, after looking at the five parked here, that someone had designed one by cutting everything they could off of a regular ground truck first. After that, they had built them from memory and spare parts, since no two here were identical. Close, but unique.

"Hello, my old friend," a man emerged from the front of the stone building.

Valentinian recognized the book dealer as the man approached. They shook hands gravely.

"Basuk," the man turned and gestured to a second man that had emerged, wearing identical, sand-colored robes. "This is the man and his friends. He is a most impressive negotiator, especially for a human."

Valentinian took that to mean that these locals weren't necessarily from around here. Not that you could tell, and he didn't care that much. Externally, they appeared to have all the right parts in the right places. And it was their planet. He was just visiting briefly.

Basuk approached and also shook hands. The man took a long moment to study the rest of the group before he smiled and turned to his cousin.

"It is good, Marduk," the man said. "You should stay and have tea with us. The shop can open late today."

The book dealer, Marduk, considered it and shrugged.

"As you command, cousin," he said lightly, giving Valentinian some visibility into their culture and their relationship.

They all filed back inside, where the air was much cooler.

"Here," Basuk said. "You can leave your heavier weapons on this rack while we talk."

There were already rifles and pistols at easy reach for anyone rushing to the front door. Valentinian nodded to the others and they stripped down to just their pistols for now, after which they trooped into a large dining space and got settled as servants began to steep tea and put out mugs and fixings.

"I understand from my cousin that you will be off to seek something in the northern, equatorial belts," Basuk said with a light smile as the tea got served. "Normally, visitors find themselves at a military disadvantage when facing the mutants of the wastes, but you appear to be both well-armed and quite capable, especially after the way you treated Rossham and his friends so roughly last night."

Valentinian shrugged.

"We are strangers here," he said with a guileless face. "Just shooting them all out of hand seemed rude. They might be related to someone important and I would hate to have to destroy this city, if the dipshit's master went and declared blood feud with me."

Valentinian liked the way both men's eyes got a

little bigger at those words. Pure bluff on his part, but they didn't need to know that. And it was only a bluff if nobody pissed him off enough to actually force the issue.

He might be the slightest bit angrier today than he had been a year ago. And surrounded by at least two killers, plus a woman who would make up for it in raw enthusiasm at this point.

"Indeed?" Basuk managed. "Well, your forbearance is noted. Not that many of the locals would have missed those men, but yes, a war in town might have spilled over onto the natives as well. Were you able to locate that which you sought in Marduk's books?"

"Perhaps," Valentinian replied, relaxing just a bit.

Dave and Kyriaki were both wound tight enough for the rest.

"According to the various sources, the place we need to go is called the Juxx Wastelands today," he continued.

"The Deep Wastes, then?" Basuk asked, his eyes growing a shade larger before they settled again. "Some of the more dangerous tribes reside there. I would recommend you avoid that area, unless your quest has religious overtones?"

"Why do you say that?" Valentinian probed.

"The mutants of that area are among the worst and weirdest of all the tribes," Marduk spoke up.

"Are they mutant, or Variant Humanity, or what?" Valentinian turned to the man.

"According to the legends we know, they were human once, as the four of you," Marduk responded. "At least as much as the Urlan overlords recognized such a thing. However, thousands of years of the heat and solar radiation of the equator have changed them. Plus there are spots where the radiation left over from the old wars is still high enough to be a threat to anyone living there for long enough."

"Radiation?"

"Once, this world was an emerald and azure paradise, my friend," Basuk said. "The Jynarri, like myself and my cousin, are native to this world, going back to the time before the Urlan Empire. Savage weapons were used to knock the planet itself out of the normal orbit and too close to our star. The results are the world-spanning deserts of the modern era. The radiation will linger for a few more millennia, at least in the worst places."

Valentinian blinked. Those wars had been theoretical things. Historical events. He had not processed that it was possible to *destroy* a world, and yet still live on it afterwards. Apparently, Kryuome was proof.

"So if we wanted to go anyway...?" Valentinian let the words linger.

"I would still recommend against it," Basuk said. "But if you are committed, you will need significant firepower. What you brought with you here was acceptable for the city, but you will need something heavier for the deep wastes."

"I noted several transports out front," Valentinian said.

"One with spare parts, if this is the size of your force," Basuk nodded. "Something monstrous to mount in the turret. I presume you would land in a secret spot and then drive to your target, lest the locals find and strip your ship while you are gone. Desert gear will be easy enough. I would recommend something extra for the females to carry at all times, so they could not be taken alive."

"Alive?" Kyriaki leaned forward and growled at the man.

Basuk nodded solemnly at her as Valentinian leaned back.

"The men would most likely just go into the stew pots if captured," the arms merchant said seriously. "The two of you would become breeding stock for the tribe. I presume that you would find that lot in life objectionable."

Valentinian wondered if Basuk was baiting the two women, which was immensely stupid, but decided after a moment that he was really trying to convey to them how dangerous it would really be out there.

Fates worse than death wasn't just a saying.

"What armaments do those tribes buy?" Dave spoke up before anyone got their feelings hurt.

"Personal arms, such as what you've brought," Basuk turned his attention to the tall killer. "They frequently have heavier gear, designed to stop an armored speeder or a low-flying craft with a missile or heavy ammunition round, such as a light auto-cannon. That is the reason my trucks have so few solid parts. The tribes are more likely to shoot at you with the smaller weapons, since the heavier might fail. At that point, it becomes a case of speed and maneuverability, and these repulsors have an edge in their weight-to-power ratios that the more heavy desert vehicles lack."

"You've equipped a number of folks for the desert," Valentinian said. It wasn't a question.

"Salvagers come regularly, seeking their

fortunes," Basuk nodded. "As do foolish historians. Some trade with the tribes. Others dislike paying transit fees, so they try to sneak in. You don't strike me as academics, in spite of your purchases at Marduk's shop. Nor are you salvagers, so I would classify you as merely adventurers. If a group such as you might be *merely* anything."

They all shared a smile and a chuckle.

Valentinian nodded after he refilled his tea.

He just might enjoy haggling with this man.

[13]
ATHANASIA

IT WAS AMAZING, what two days and a heavy dose of *personal awakening* might do to someone. Athanasia studied Stephaneria's new persona with a warm smile.

Gone was the demure librarian in the long skirt, her hair up sensibly. Today she was in black. Leggings, tunic, tabard, done with a dark crimson almost maroon as highlights, edging, and flashing. Her hair was down and tousled. Her eyes were no longer polite.

Athanasia wore a similar outfit, something considered normal fashion within the Dominion Household, but hers was gray and gold, as befit the Dowager wife of the Dominator, however few people might ever realize that, this many hundreds of light-years from home.

They were both armed today as well. Shock pistols on their belts, just in case, but Athanasia relied more on the team of killers lining the walls of this small chamber as she and Stephaneria sat at a conference table in a space at the station library.

Stephaneria had given her notice, and would depart the station in another few days, but she still had all her contacts here. Friends who might pass along rumors and stories. Access to dangerous men, like the one Athanasia expected shortly.

The door opened and the M'Rai captain ducked under the sill to enter.

He was three meters tall and muscular. Not as well organized as her former husband, but the man still had a V-shape to his torso, even as his stomach had a bit of a paunch going.

She didn't need to seduce the man physically, however interesting such a coupling might prove. They had apparently been designed to be more or less compatible with smaller humans.

Rage emanated off the man, in waves similar to Stephaneria at those moments when she got introspective. Interestingly, and by the sheerest luck Athanasia that didn't believe in, the same man had been the cause with both of them.

"Sit, Captain Vidy-Wooders," Athanasia more or less ordered the man.

Best to establish the terms of the relationship right now. He would no doubt rebel and resist, but let him strain the leash against her after she had put it upon him.

The M'Rai giant glowered at her from under heavy brows, but took a seat across from them. Stephaneria had even found a chair that would fit the man, and a table that could be adjusted so everyone was comfortable. The two women's feet dangled, but it made this a meeting of more-or-less equals.

"Do you know who I am?" Athanasia queried him sharply.

"An Ambassador from someplace called Dominion," Vidy-Wooders spit out harshly.

"Close," she corrected him. "A hunter. Dave Hall was my husband, before he abandoned me and fled justice aboard a ship named *Longshot Hypothesis*, captained by a man you apparently know."

It was almost pleasant, watching both of them twitch at the thought of Captain Tarasicodissa.

"Go on," the man growled.

"I have a lead to where they went, after Begzatlari," Athanasia smiled coldly at him. "After your encounter with the man. It's a pity you don't have a crew these days, or a warship, or I might hire you to assist my vengeance."

He reared back a little before he caught himself. She heard grumbles under his breath.

"You have a warship?" he asked.

"I have a Dominion Assault Courier at my command," she corrected him again. "And a crew. You have an unarmed salvage transport, and you are alone."

"Why am I here?" he asked heavily.

"You want to be avenged on those people almost as much as I do," she tried to be charming, in spite of her opinion on the salvager. "And you have a much better understanding of Wildspace. I want to see if we can reach an accommodation."

"What kind?" his eyes had a warmer glow now.

"I'll give you the coordinates where I intend to go," she replied. "My ship's faster than yours, so I'll get there first. Plus, I have guns and a crew, so I might be able to kill Dave Hall when I get there."

"And if not?" he leaned forward enough to rest his elbows and hands on the table.

"Then the hunt will take a very long time," Athanasia studied the man closer. "My former masters won't let me go after him forever. My crew will rebel at some point, so I will need to hire a ship. An armed privateer with a new crew, but I'll require a bloodhound who knows Wildspace. A pilot who can track them down, and wants them as bad as I do. You strike me as that kind of man."

She watched his body language now as the man *considered* her offer.

He could get even with Tarasicodissa, and with his own former crew member who had apparently broken into the ship to steal all her gear back. At the same time, this proud man would have to submit to a woman. Suborn himself.

She doubted the man needed money. Rumors had circulated about the cargo that had been valuable enough to dump his crew at Bohrne Station, the last time he had come through.

Did his anger outweigh his greed and his pride?

Athanasia reached out with a hand and ran it through Stephaneria's hair. Listened to the woman growl with emotion. It wasn't a sexual display intended to arouse the man, but a show of dominance to cow him. To show him what vengeance might taste like, if he was willing to submit.

It helped that his reputation in Laurentia was already so low. Word had gotten around that the man had abandoned his former crew rather than pay them. Only the most desperate people would be willing to hire on to his ship now.

That was just another thing she could use to bait her trap.

"Well?" Athanasia turned back to the M'Rai giant and pinned his psyche to the wall like a dead butterfly.

"I will meet you there," he finally said, huskily.

"Good," she smiled, rising to shake his hand. "I will have the coordinates transmitted to your ship shortly. And then we can begin to hunt."

She could never return to what she had before. Even in the Dominion she would be an afterthought. But with his reputation in tatters, neither could this man.

In Wildspace, however, she could take the funds that had been intended to keep her away for a very long time, and perhaps turn herself into a pirate. A warlord. She would need angry, dangerous people to catch her prey.

There was no reason to let such a crew go to waste after she had killed Hall. And the M'Rai had the makings of the perfect minion for her later.

[14]
KYRIAKI

She didn't like it, but she wasn't in charge. Kyriaki could take measures to mitigate the risk, however. Right now, that meant that Valentinian drove their new truck. Dave sat with a good firing arc forward and right, covering things with that rifle of his. Bayjy had the left with her plasma rifle.

Kyriaki had claimed the turret, after Basuk had ordered his men to drop a twin pulse cannon into the ring.

Let's just see what that fool Rossham and his master wanted to try today.

They had taken a short run out into the nearby wastes with Basuk and a mechanic aboard, to confirm how everything worked. The engines and maneuverability had been sufficient to impress the captain.

She'd gotten to unleash hell on a rock facing, testing the extra generator that had been purchased and added specifically to power such a nasty weapon. Kyriaki wasn't quite good enough to sign her name with the cannon. At least not today.

If they ended up in a running firefight with a tribe of crazed, cannibalistic, sex fiends, that might change.

Valentinian drove the sled back to the compound and lowered it onto the landing gear.

"Yes," he said simply, pulling a wad of bills from a pocket and handing them to the arms dealer with a harsh grin the man reciprocated as he and the mechanic climbed out.

"I am so glad we were able to do business, Captain Tarasicodissa," Basuk stepped back and bowed. He looked up at Kyriaki next. "And if you choose to seek other employment, dangerous lady, please contact me first and I will find you the best jobs on the planet."

After three hours with the locals, she understood the level of compliment intended. She nodded with a half-shrug. If it came to that, she was in much deeper trouble than just being unemployed.

Valentinian lifted the sled back up and banked around to the left, opening the throttle a little as they circled the city and climbed onto the distant plateau at high speed.

Kyriaki saw the man first, since she was flying up top with heavy goggles that protected much of her face, and the targeting reticle of the twins hovering in the air on their laser.

Longshot Hypothesis sat out in the open, for the most part, once you got to the top of the bluff. A man was sitting a polite distance away from the ship in a folding chair with a solar umbrella proving some shade. She yelled a warning to Valentinian and rotated the guns to look for other targets. Dave would have the man's eyeball, even at this range and at speed. Kyriaki had seen that deadly killer move on Tartarus.

But nothing presented itself in the way of assholes needing to be killed today.

"Bayjy," Valentinian called over the harsh buzz of the repulsors and the wind. "Are the alarms all still active?"

"Stand by," the purple nemesis called, putting her rifle down and pulling out her cardreader. That woman knew more about security systems than any of the other three of them, maybe combined, and they could all break into most places. Bayjy would simply snap her fingers and the systems would turn themselves off for her.

"We're intact, Captain," Bayjy said after a few seconds. "Somebody rang the doorbell, and then nothing."

"Remind me to add a signal to our cardreaders in the future," Valentinian said. "Send us a notification when that happens, anywhere we might be in range. Plus zero a camera in so we can see who it is."

"Piece of cake," Bayjy laughed.

They were getting close to the man waiting, so Valentinian slowed to a polite speed and then finally stopped. Kyriaki lined him up with the twin pulse cannon anyway, even as she locked the weapon down, dropped out of the ring, pulled her assault pulsar out and hopped off the side of the vehicle.

Fortunately, this man was a stranger, and not somebody she would be duty-bound to annihilate right now. Pity, she supposed, but at least the man who had been sent last night had either learned his lesson, or had competition.

"Captain?" the man rose and bowed.

He was wearing the robes that everyone wore if they spent any time outdoors on this planet. Sand colored and well draped. Expensive-looking, too.

Valentinian shut the craft down and climbed out, as did the others. She glanced over and smiled when Dave switched to overwatch, that killing rifle sniffing the aim for snipers about to try something. That left her free to talk to this person.

She walked to about four meters away and centered her weapon on his chest with a hungry smile. She had practiced that look, back when she wore the white beret, as a way to intimidate the hell out of everyone.

It still worked. He swallowed loudly and flinched.

"Here," Valentinian stepped closer and studied the man. "Who are you?"

"A messenger, sir," the fool managed weakly. "Truqtok was unhappy that yesterday's courier was found unacceptable, so I was sent in his place."

She eyeballed the man closer now, noting that this Truqtok fellow had either sent his lawyer, or his chief of staff. Not one of yesterday's killers. Somebody with brains. Possibly the only other person in the gang, if it was like most criminal organizations.

They tended to be long on thugs and short on intelligence, until you got to the top and found the men and women who used pens instead of shock pistols to commit their crimes.

"I see," Valentinian said crisply. "After yesterday, you won't be offended if I don't invite you inside for tea. However, nor will I cast your corpse into the desert wastes. How may I be of service?"

Kyriaki nearly did a double-take, watching Valentinian turn into someone else before her eyes. All morning he had been a hard-as-nails pirate captain. Now he was a Dominion gentleman.

Weird. But she knew the man could be a chameleon. It was just educational to watch it in action. Nobody she had ever known could shift so smoothly, and she had arrested and extradited some of the best conmen around in her time.

"When you were unavailable this morning, I was instructed to await your return," the man said. "My master would congress with you, at your convenience."

Valentinian literally clicked his heels together and bent forty-five degrees at the waist, as if they were on a government floor.

"Very good," her captain replied. "As you can see, we have just returned from a shopping trip, and will need some time to stow everything correctly aboard. Then it will be the hottest part of the day. Perhaps we could meet an hour before sunset?"

"That would be acceptable, Captain," the man bowed back.

She perked up when a hand dipped into a pocket, but he withdrew a card, rather than a weapon, and held it out lightly.

"Directions to Truqtok's compound, west of the city, Captain," he said. "I will convey your estimated arrival to my principal and we will look forward to entertaining you."

He turned with a nod to her and the rest and walked back down the trail as if there were no weapons at all trained on his back. Kyriaki looked over at Valentinian, but he shook his head and started back the other way.

"Bayjy, open her up," Valentinian called as he climbed back into the rig.

She and Dave covered everything else that might move, until the sound of the desert sled grew silent inside the big cargo bay. She went in last and closed the big doors with a palm on the switch, watching the waning crack until the outside heat was blocked and air conditioning flowed.

"I swear you people like living at the south pole," Bayjy groused loudly as she headed forward to grab warmer clothes.

They met up again in the lounge upstairs as Bayjy pulled on a hooded sweatshirt and extra socks.

"We going to meet this warlord punk?" Kyriaki asked as they settled.

"Don't really have much choice here," Valentinian nodded. "Good ones, anyway. Meet with him tonight, or blast off right now for the deep desert and try to hide from whatever agents might be there."

"It's a trap," Bayjy opined. "Y'all know that, right?"

"They all are, Bayjy," Valentinian agreed.

Kyriaki nodded with both of them. But what choice did they have, other than to walk in ready to kill everyone that moved and hope that it was enough?

Kyriaki would handle her part, if it came down to death and mayhem.

[15]
GLAXU

By the time Glaxu had landed *Outermost* in a nearby canyon and gotten the ship covered by a desert tarp, the sun was mid-morning, which should have made his approach easy. The humans would be down in the city for a time yet. Their kind never walked long distances in the sun unless they had to.

But there was someone else watching the new ship when he slipped over the crest of the ridgeline. Local. One he knew by reputation, although they had never personally met.

Ehlgeron. Truqtok's fixer. Dangerous, dangerous man.

Immediately, Glaxu had gone for cover, then he carefully stalked forward as if a dozen snipers were waiting for him to appear. Interestingly, the man had a camp chair to sit on, and his signature solar umbrella.

And patience, apparently. The human was sitting in a place where Glaxu could sneak up on him, if necessary, but not the ship. He appeared happy to wait for the other humans to return.

So much for trying to crack the security systems and steal what he needed.

Glaxu found a good perch mostly behind the man, once he circled around and confirmed that Ehlgeron was here alone. Today, Glaxu had worn his desert shorts, baggy enough to run if he needed to, but with nests on each side where he could put eggs or other valuables as needed.

The shock pistol was under his left wing on the crossed bandolier, with a vibroblade on the right side. Other equipment was stashed in pockets on the bandolier or on his greaves where he could get at things in a hurry.

Because he was in a mood this morning, Glaxu had also added the shock bracers around the outside of his greaves, just above the ankle joint. That would let him just take a human down in a fight, when his natural instinct would be a dewclaw rake that opened up flesh. These people never wore any form of armor against blades.

Fools.

His shorts weren't as good as a squatting cloth, but he needed to be prepared to move at high speed in a heartbeat, and the cloth always risked tripping him.

The costs of style.

Ehlgeron waited like a hunter, so Glaxu did as well. He had on a leather cap to protect the sides of his head against bugs and dust, and pulled his goggles down over his eyes, letting the electronics inside measure the exact distance to the fixer. The altitude. Temperature. Barometric pressure. Weather forecast. Available radio stations by musical format. Exact vector back to *Outermost*.

After an hour, Glaxu finally grinned. The human stood and walked around the ship once, probably to stretch his legs. The man was middle-aged, as humans went, so he probably needed to exercise more. Or he was confirming that no other ambushers besides an ambitious Mondi had snuck up on him.

There was that.

Ehlgeron sat again, pulling out his cardreader and losing himself in business, probably. Glaxu continued to watch.

He heard the ship's crew returning. He hoped it was them, and not a fourth party coming to the spring mating dances.

A desert speeder was coming up from the left at high speed. Rather than move his head and risk drawing attention, Glaxu let his peripheral vision track the machine. One of the ones he had seen earlier when overflying, from the shape.

A box covered over with just enough mesh for humans in boots to stand on. He would find it uncomfortable, trying to hold on with zygodactyl toes, unless the designer had somehow picked a mesh scale that he could wrap toes around like a damned parrot on a branch.

Four humans. The same four that had departed the ship this morning as he had flown above. They paused outside the ship and spoke with the fixer as Glaxu listened in, hiding in the rocks brown on brown. Retired to within the ship as Ehlgeron returned to the city.

The vehicle suggested a trip to the deserts where even Mondi were careful not to tread. At the same time, Truqtok's man was treating them with wary respect, so perhaps they were dangerous enough to take care of themselves.

The desert speeder was certainly well armed, over and above the four humans.

Still, they had something he wanted. Needed. If he waited until they left, Truqtok might have more killers in the area. Alternatively, they might decide to flee immediately, rather than deal with any local troubles, and he would be reduced to chasing them across the planet.

Glaxu replayed the tapes. Yesterday's messenger? So Ehlgeron was the fallback after Truqtok probably sent his bully boys. And they had made it home safe, or Truqtok would have sent an army today.

That suggested that maybe he was dealing with more civilized folk that was normal for this planet.

He could work with that. And time was short.

Glaxu rose and approached the rear of the vessel with a jaunty stride.

[16]

VALENTINIAN

THE DOORBELL RINGING had Valentinian out of his chair, with a heavy flamer in his hands, and three steps away from the table before his brain engaged. Happily, the other three were only about a step behind him.

Unhappily, they all plowed into him from behind when he tried to stop. Somehow, nobody ended up going down the staircase face first in the process of getting halted.

"Good," Valentinian announced, holstering his pistol. "Glad I'm not the only one a little too wound up."

That generated a laugh.

"Dave, you get to the bridge and check sensors," he ordered. "Kyriaki with me. Bayjy stay back at the bottom of the stairs to shoot anybody if they make it past us. Questions?"

A moment of thought, and then bodies exploded into motion.

Valentinian jogged to the aft airlock and flipped

on the screen to show their visitor. He was assuming it was the man, returned with some message or update.

That or a deadly surprise as someone tried to rush the door. Which was why Bayjy had a plasma rifle in her hands. That sort of weapon didn't require pinpoint accuracy, especially when someone had to come through a two-meter-wide hatch to get to you.

Valentinian was not prepared for the image that greeted him.

He was familiar with ostriches. There were a few planets in the Dominion where the creatures ran wild. Plus numerous zoos he had visited as a kid.

The person at the door was an ostrich. Sort of. In miniature, maybe.

About a meter tall, with long legs and a long neck. Short, stubby body in the middle. Beak instead of a mouth, long and heavy, coming down to a chisel point rather than slender like a hummingbird. Two big eyes with copper-colored irises were fixed forward, like a predator, rather than on the sides, like prey.

Dark brown feathers on his back and head, running a lighter brown on his neck before fading to cream on the creature's belly.

It was an intelligent being. He (he?) wore shorts, spats, a bandolier, and a leather hat with goggles pushed up. Signs of technology, especially his pistol in a shoulder holster, if the being had shoulders. Stubby arms. Long legs.

The pistol was not in a feathered hand. So whoever it was wanted to talk, presumably.

"Dave," Valentinian said into the intercom. "Is he alone?"

"Affirmative, Vee," Dave replied. "Only two things moving are the guy leaving and the one at the hatch. And the first man is leaving. Just got past the point where we had our fun last night."

"Good," Valentinian raised his voice. "Opening the aft hatch."

Kyriaki was several steps back and off to one side, mostly obscured by a hardsuit hanging on a rack. Valentinian figured he was safe with her covering things, so put his pistol away and keyed the hatch to open, stepping back at he did.

The system beeped politely and then opened.

The creature waited outside at a polite distance. He had an odd smell Valentinian couldn't place. Brighter than cinnamon, but Valentinian wasn't enough of a cook to identify it, other than he was pretty sure it was in his kitchen, if he wanted to track it down later.

The creature put his feet together and bowed over clasped hands.

"Greetings, fellow travelers," it said in a warm, baritone voice that sounded like it should have come from a much larger person.

"Hello," Valentinian bowed back. Proper Dominion manners weren't all that different. "What brings you to Kryuome?"

Neither of them moved one bit forward.

"Unfortunately, a broken warp array controller," the creature said. "I am Redtip Windrunner Oedressa *Farther* Glaxu."

It took Valentinian a second to break that down into names, rather than gibberish.

"Captain Valentinian Tarasicodissa," he replied. "I'm human. What species do you represent?"

"Mondi," the man said with a nod. "We are rare in this octant of space."

That was an understatement. To date, Valentinian had never met an alien that wasn't close enough to human for government work. Even the three meter tall M'Rai qualified, as they could occasionally hybridize with one of the smaller Variant Humanities. This man's ancestors had been land birds, rather than jungle apes.

"Ah." Valentinian nodded, still not moving. "Not one I am familiar with, but I come from a great distance spinward, myself."

"Spinward?" the Mondi asked. "Interesting. There are rumors of civilized star empires beyond Wildspace in that direction."

"Laurentia," Valentinian nodded. "Asherah. Qetesh. Lie-Zu. The Dominion."

"Do you have a warp mechanic I might hire for a day or two?" the creature asked, just like a Dominion gentleman.

Valentinian felt himself falling back into those rituals.

"Not a dedicated one, per se," he shrugged. "However, we have some level of technical expertise aboard. Would you care to join us for tea?"

It was a little off-putting, watching that tiny head cock one way, and then the other. After a moment, Valentinian realized that it would be the same as him turning side-eye on a situation, trying to gauge risk. Or a dog sniffing for trouble.

"It would be extremely rude of me to invite myself aboard your ship, Captain," the visitor finally exclaimed.

And highly risky, if I wanted to take you prisoner

and sell or ransom you off to someone, yes. Still, we can act like civilized creatures, at least for a time.

"Indeed, good sir," Valentinian let the imprinted patterns of Gymnasia Dominia come to the fore.

Once upon a time, he had been training to become an officer in the Dominion Armada. Before that unfortunate misunderstanding with smuggled goods. Where things ended up that he was the only person left when everyone else had someone important to hide behind, leaving him as the scapegoat.

"If you would give me a moment, I will ask my crew to make preparations, and then I will join you out in the shade and we can chat like civilized folk."

"Very good, Captain," the Mondi bowed again and moved off to the part of the yard where *Longshot* cast a nice shadow.

Valentinian turned to Kyriaki with a smile and a shrug.

"Cold tea, please?" he asked.

"You are completely insane, Valentinian," she shook her head to herself.

"That's beside the point, Kyriaki," he said. "Sailor in need. There are rules and customs that civilized people are expected to follow. Shape does not factor into it at any point."

"Understood," she actually smiled at him. "Just stating the obvious."

"Hey," he said as she started to turn. "I can be helpless and harmless these days. I've got the three of you backing me up. The rest is just a show."

That got through to her. She smiled a little and nodded.

Valentinian exited through the airlock and closed it behind him.

"Redtip Windrunner Oedressa *Farther* Glaxu?" Valentinian asked as he joined the smaller man, bird, person, whatever, in the shade.

"Correct, Captain," the Mondi nodded, his eyes growing larger. "Most humans require several attempts to get it right. Thank you."

"What is the naming structure?" the nearly-Dominion officer and gentleman asked, speaking with Valentinian's tongue.

"Tribe, clan, family, nickname, and personal name," the Mondi said. "I would thus be Captain Oedressa to strangers, and *Farther* to the other pilots of my nest."

"*Farther*?" Valentinian asked.

"My ship is named *Outermost*, Captain," he said. "Always the closest to the enemy in our flying formations. I was the one that wanted to remain in this octant of space, when the others voted to return to our home sectors. It was the black humor of the gods that my ship suffered the malfunction that left me adrift in this place just as the others got up to speed."

"I see," Valentinian replied. "I am in similar circumstances. My crew are all a long ways from their homes, but not likely to return in the near future."

He heard beeping as someone opened the hatch and emerged.

Bayjy, stripped of her extra socks and sweatshirt and most likely reveling in life at a low broil, in her shorts and a tight T-shirt.

"Captains," she said with a saucy smile as she

approached, a pitcher in one hand, two mugs in the other, and the plasma rifle slung across her back.

Kyriaki had also emerged, standing at the rear hatch and ignoring the rest of them to keep watch. Dave was either still in the cockpit or up top with the sniper rifle.

It was nice, not having to worry about anything except the strange birdman in front of him.

They both took mugs, Captain Oedressa requiring both hands, since it was so large. Bayjy poured and smiled, stepping back and pointedly stood in the direct sunlight, like a lizard on the perfect rock.

Valentinian started sweating just watching her.

"So, if you are a stranger to the zones known as Wildspace, will the technology be close enough for us to be able to repair, or adapt parts?" Valentinian asked after a few sips of the cold heaven.

A Mondi shrug apparently involved the palms rotating up and out, with the body pitching slightly forward at the hips. At least, if Valentinian was reading the man's body language correctly. Always an iffy topic, when suddenly dealing with a true alien, and not a close-enough-biped with different internal chemistry. It was doubly interesting watching him do that and still not manage to spill any of the tea.

"It is my fervent hope, Captain," he said. "I have attempted to engage locals, but most of them are incapable of diagnosing such advanced technology. At a certain point, I ran somewhat afoul of the local power structure and found it necessary to depart the city for safer climates."

"Truqtok?" Valentinian asked, wondering if this man, this bird represented a third option.

Basuk had held a low opinion of the humans around here, but the two species kept largely to themselves. If Valentinian had been out at night the first time, he probably would have never spoke that much with the Jynarri.

"Some of his band of people, yes," Captain Oedressa nodded. "After winning several duels with his thugs, I apparently enraged them."

Valentinian studied the man closer now. Half his height. At most a quarter of his weight. But the way he stood suggested a kick-fighter, especially the bit where he was wearing spats, rather than boots, exposing clawed toes, and had metal and cloth greaves close to his ankles. The pockets on them did an exceptional job of disguising their purpose, but he suspected it would be like a human with a cestus on each hand when punching.

"I see," Valentinian grinned.

They shared a secret joke, and Oedressa nodded deep enough to almost constitute a bow.

"Were you present enough to overhear my conversation with the earlier visitor?" Valentinian asked. He assumed, but it was worth seeing if the tiny killer would admit it.

"I was," Oedressa noted. "I found it relevant enough to witness, just in case, although I hope you will not take offense."

"None, in fact," Valentinian bowed in turn. "But I have just spent a morning with Basuk, the Jynarri arms merchant, and he has a similarly low opinion of the human tribes in this town. I would not like to depart from my ship's current location at present. Could you retrieve yours and join us here?"

"Rather quickly, actually," Oedressa grinned.

A Mondi grin was all eyes and a slight head cock, since the beak was rigid. But the body language was obvious, if you were listening.

"However," the birdman continued. "I suspect repairs will take far longer to complete."

Valentinian grinned now.

"As you know, I have an appointment with Truqtok later today," he said smoothly. "Perhaps you would care to join us, in some sort of a vague, bodyguarding capacity?"

"Unless you have truly angered that human, I cannot imagine you would need it," Oedressa noted somewhat evasively. "And in that case, I doubt my presence would mitigate things."

"True," Valentinian agreed. "But it would give you a vested interest in our success, that we might be able to more quickly turn towards repairing your vessel."

Those huge eyes blinked. Twice. Zeroed in on him hard.

A Mondi laugh was rather like a big cat chuffing, Valentinian learned.

"Well played, Captain," Oedressa chuckled. "I accept your invitation. His men already know to fear me, so you may inherit some of that wrath, I must warn you."

"I do not plan to remain on this planet any longer than absolutely necessary," Valentinian admitted in a hard voice. "And then to never look back. But I can take the time to help get you into space again."

"Thank you," Oedressa bowed formally again and stepped back. He turned to Bayjy and bowed to her as well. "Madam, the tea was excellent. If you will excuse me, I must run to retrieve my ship. I will see you again in a few hours."

Valentinian watched a wary Bayjy accept the mug from the tiny man.

The Mondi took two strides away and he was already moving at thirty kph. Two more and he was closer to sixty, if Valentinian could judge it accurately.

Ground bird. Hunter from the placement of his eyes. Really damned fast when he wanted to show off. Or remind the pitiful humans that they couldn't keep up with him on their best day.

Valentinian filed that for reference.

"You're nuts," Bayjy echoed Kyriaki.

"Tell me something I don't know?" Valentinian asked her.

"He's cute, and deadly," she tried. "We really taking him with us?"

"Depends on him," Valentinian said. "Now, let's get back inside where you can put some clothes on and I can plan while we eat."

She winked at him and he was certain the extra wiggle in her bottom was an invitation, if he wanted to pursue it. Not quite the stupidest idea in the galaxy, but probably not all that far away from it. Tight pants and shirt on the woman didn't help his frame of mind.

Still, he had work to do, and a good crew.

Now if he could just stay out of local troubles.

[17]

GLAXU

Glaxu really couldn't take offense at the situation he found himself in. The human had played an exceptional, metaphorical match of jousting and caught him from below and behind with his lance. Glaxu was just amazed that the human had arrived at how to maneuver them into that situation.

Most humans were two-dimensional fighters, which made a pitiful kind of sense, since they had never managed to fly before technological assistance. The Mondi had lost most of their ability over the ages, but still retained the instincts, and had honed them once they had ships that could fly for them again.

He was just glad that he had been thwarted in his earlier plans to merely break in and try to steal the parts he needed. Glaxu knew he was no great mechanical engineer. And Captain Tarasicodissa had been revealed to be both brutal and civilized.

It would be interesting, entering Truqtok's throne room for the first time in the company of the four human strangers. At once, he would be part of a nest again, however temporarily, and that appeared to be part of the *quid pro quo* that the captain would insist upon for the technical assistance.

Truly, a masterful performance. Glaxu decided to leave the shock bracers on when he joined them later. Perhaps one of the thugs could be enticed to dance, and Glaxu could give his new friends an example of just how dangerous the little bird hunter really was, just in case they were entertaining piratical thoughts.

He would hate to have to kill all of them, right after they had done him the favor of fixing his ship.

Up and over the fifth rise, he found the lip above the little box canyon where *Outermost* was stashed. Even humans would be hard pressed to imagine that you could stash a flying craft in there. Repulsorlift craft like Captain Tarasicodissa had apparently just purchased were barely smaller, and usually lacked the fine, vertical control of a Mondi fightership.

Glaxu danced along the edge for a few yards, inspecting the space below, and then hopped off the cliff, fluttering and gliding for the eight meters to the top of his ship, hidden below a tarp that honestly made it look like desert floor, even before all the shadows.

Quickly, he detached the elastic cords from the various hooks with his toes, walking backwards and rolling it up as he went. *Outermost* emerged as he did so, the black and gray hull lurking at the bottom of the valley like a puma trapped in a well.

The tarps went into storage nests forward from the engines and sealed for space flight. He popped open the hatch between the engines and walked forward, happy to be back on the old, wooden floors that just felt so much more right. Past the Larder and all his various food stuffs he had been able to supplement with local snakes. Past the Branch where his compact turds got stored and processed. Forward from the Cactus where he slept, at least while in flight.

Glaxu had taken to sleeping under the ship occasionally, just because this stupid planet did remind him so much of home.

Finally, he squatted down onto his flight saddle and stretched his legs forward. Glaxu was simply unable to envision how the pitiful humans could fly and fight at the same time, without using their feet, but they managed. And some of them were even at an acceptable rate of expertise.

At least as long as they weren't engaging his full nest in deep space fracas. Then they were usually in over their heads, which was the risk you chose when you went into space.

Preflight didn't take long. He had shut the ship down carefully when he parked here, expecting to be a while if he had to sneak up on someone.

Outermost responded to power with a warm, happy hum, and Glaxu pulled back on the control yoke. Straight up the well the puma climbed, emerging into the sunlight with an angry growl.

It was a short flight, but he felt like pushing the envelope a little, so Glaxu rotated the ship's geometry into a form he rarely used, looking something like an ocean ray with the forward canards to full, lateral extension and the main wings rotated as far forward as they would go and then slid out.

This shape gave him a lift capability that was

stupendous, compared to his more combat-ready forms, at a cost of speed, but he was less than a three kilometers from the human camp already. He lit the engines and idled over to the humans like a hungry ray.

After all, they had probably never seen a Mondi fightership in their lives. They would need to appreciate how dangerous it could be.

Just like the pilot.

SHE KINDA LAUGHED when she thought about it, but kept her face all stern and stuff. Bayjy Endon: gun-toting, ass-kicking, pirate babe.

Sure.

Captain liked to talk about no longer having to be a killer, with the three of them around, but she had no doubts about how dangerous that boy could be when pressed. She'd seen death take up residence in those blue-green eyes a time or two.

And adding the cute birdman hadn't altered that equation. She was still the least dangerous person here, even with a short-range plasma rifle strapped on her hip. Kyrie was ex-cop with all that martial arts training. And Big Guy was seriously the ex-Dominator, on the run from his ex-wife and whole empire?

Bayjy let a little grin slip out. Maybe her nose scrunched a little bit with the humor. She could pass it off as a response to the endearing attempts of these other punks to look tough around them. She could even give them lessons, but then she'd sailed with Butler Vidy-Wooders for a couple of years before this crew.

She understood how to project it like a fire hose.

Captain had parked the sled in the driveway out front when they arrived. And he'd driven down the hill slow enough that everybody got just a little wind-whipped, but not sanded down.

Everyone around here was either wearing desert robes, or had gone for that standard spacer look men apparently ordered out of the same catalog: tall boots, tight pants tucked in, light shirt tucked in, and either a vest or a jacket.

Did this Truqtok dude have a contract with Central Casting to handle extras and costuming?

At least she'd known that there would be air conditioning in this small hellhole, so she'd fallen back on her heatsuit under the sort of pants and shirt that guaranteed most men never remembered the color of her eyes, if they even noticed she had a face in the first place.

Kyrie actually had a better butt, but that girl was too self-conscious about it most of the time to use it as a weapon. Unless she was going after Captain. Totally different story there.

Bayjy led, because screw you people. All of you.

She sauntered through the big double doors like a princess returning from a year at war and sniffing aloud at the failure of the help to keep the place clean. A couple of the men looked like they might take umbrage. She marked them for an extra, sneering smile as she went by.

And it was all men in here. Stupid, chauvinistic punks with no idea how dangerous a woman might be, if you handed her a gun or a length of pipe. Based on the grumblings from little Glaxu on the ride in, it was even worse when you weren't human.

She caught the murmurings when he entered fourth, behind Big Guy and Captain and ahead of Kyrie. Hopefully, these fools caught the significance of the two women being at the guard positions on the ends of the column.

Probably not. Probably they were too busy studying the way her boobs swayed as she walked. They'd never note that she held one, possessive hand on the cold chrome finish of her plasma rifle, just waiting for some lunkhead to need to be chunked into a wall with it.

The locals had opened up a pathway, which Bayjy mostly followed, taking her time and memorizing the layout, just in case Captain let her come back later and break their electronic security systems down into alarm clocks and pocket toys.

Not much looked worth stealing in here. Other than Truqtok's peace of mind.

There was always that. She smiled, and suddenly realized why Captain had put her up front, instead of the hard, endless scowls Kyrie was probably sending downrange.

You sneaky bastard.

She grinned some more. Watched it ripple out across these fool pirates like an electric shock that zapped them one by one.

Down three broad, shallow steps into a bigger room. Bayjy paid attention to the floor as she walked, but it was all stone here. She'd been aboard a wreck once where the captain of the ship had set up a couple of trapdoors in the floor of his main office.

Her guess had been that everyone sat in a chair on one, and the Urlan bastard in charge could drop you into cages below if he got pissed. Or scared.

She wouldn't put it past this shitbird here, but she was also the person most likely to prepare for such a trap. So Captain had her on point.

Damn, that man had a twisted mind behind those cute eyes.

Space cleared out here. Throne at one end, but only up two steps, so maybe more of a platform than a dais. Big, ugly true human seated. Lawyer-dude was off to one side. Gun-thug of some Variant flavor on the other side.

No sign of the six dipshits she'd met before, so maybe Boss-dude had a clue about provoking Captain into carrying out his threat to squish them fools like bugs.

Bayjy flipped a coin in her head and drifted to the right so the rest of the line could stretch out. That would put Kyrie opposite the lawyer, who was probably the most dangerous person in here, looking at the rest. Let the fool mess with her cop.

They were just the sorts of human specist punks you found underground in shitholes like this. Hell, they probably considered her an alien. Not that she had any intentions of proving that she was one hundred percent woman.

Not with these losers.

No, she just smiled up at the Boss-dude and the Gun-thug like she was measuring them for coffins. Granted, if that happened, she probably *was* the one person here who knew how to build a coffin correctly from scrap, but that was a whole 'nother story.

Big Dude moved quieter than any being Bayjy

had ever met, so he just kind of appeared from nothing in her peripheral vision with that longrifle in one hand. Not that she'd expected them to vanish, leaving her alone down here like that nightmare where you are about to walk into an airlock for the next cutter mission and realize that you're stark naked in a haunted ship.

Still, it was nice to have reassurances.

Captain wasn't much noisier when he moved. Nor Kyrie. Seriously, only Glaxu made a sound, that eerie clacking when his claws scraped stone.

He had added the cutest booties on the drive down, explaining that movement on stone was risky without them. His feet were X-shaped, so the things he put on looked like fingerless gloves, letting him grip better with the balls of his feet, while still being able to hook toes on the floor of the repulsor, or, as he explained it, ripping someone's throat out with all eight toes in a pinch, since the dewclaw was covered under the shock bracers he wore on his ankles.

Nifty piece of work. And his tailor must have been a stud, to take that shape and make it all work.

As a woman who had to fit everything over a heatsuit, or bury herself under layers of warm when she couldn't, Bayjy appreciated the radical importance of good tailoring.

"I had not realized the Mondi was part of your operation, Captain," Truqtok began without preamble.

He had a rough voice. Like maybe he stuffed acorns in his mouth before he talked. High pitched, too. Probably higher than hers, although she wasn't about to point that out in here. Or laugh at the man and provoke him.

Yet.

They were bullies. You laughed at those suckers. That disturbed their whole pecking order, because weakness meant blood, like a pack of sharks.

"He's a most effective scout," Captain replied with a grin in his voice. "Small, fast, and dangerous, so he can sniff out trouble ahead of time. Then we come in and back him up."

Huh. Put the fear of God into these punks. Or at least fear of Glaxu. Made sense if they went their separate ways later, to make the locals think the Mondi had backup he could call.

Captain really was a sneaky shit, wasn't he? Those poker games were no fluke.

"When you arrived on Kryuome, you didn't engage with the humans, Captain," the warlord stated. Maybe asked. It was hard to tell with that voice. "Only the aliens."

"Didn't realize that there was a split," Valentinian replied with a long, slow drawl, like honey first thing in the morning for your coffee. "Although as near as I can tell, they're the locals and we're aliens on this planet."

That provoked a sound from the mob around them. Not a groan. Not a growl. Something.

Bayjy fixed the nearest dude for a swift knee to the groin if he moved towards her. And smiled at him as she did.

"Plus, I don't plan to be here long," Captain continued. "Needed some supplies and gear, and then heading south to the pole to do some salvage work."

"There's nothing at the poles," Truqtok growled back. "They've never been inhabited. Even before."

"Not what the old records say," Captain breezed at the crowd. "Some sort of secret, Urlan Base left over from the wars. I had a different scout than Redtip confirm that it's never even been cracked open."

Different groan this time. Tasted like suppressed avarice. Like maybe these poor boys had been sitting on top of a gold mine all this time and never realized it.

South Pole was a nice touch, too. Get them all out of Captain's hair while he went off to deal with the Muties up north.

Bayjy glanced over at the trio on the platform. They might not be buying it, but their crew sure was. Captain Tarasicodissa was pretty damned good at this.

"Anyone salvaging on my planet pays a tithe," Truqtok snarled.

"Huh," Captain's voice suddenly had a cruel edge she hadn't heard before. "Nobody mentioned it was your planet. This just happened to be the city where we set down for supplies. There are several other, bigger places we could have chosen. Mistook this place for civilized, when it turns out the locals can barely read."

Even different sound. Angrier this time. What was the old saying? A hurt dog will howl.

Captain must have hit a little too close to home with that jibe.

Bayjy let her right hand slide down the rifle a little more. Not into the trigger well, but touching it with her pinkie, in case she needed to shoot someone. Safety had been off since the moment the truck landed out front.

"You'll still pay, boyo," Truqtok growled.

"Maybe," Captain breezed back at the dude. "And maybe I'll go visit Basuk's cousin in Soulrake and ask them if they recognize you as planetary governor."

Cold threat, that one. Like a big rock dropped into warm mud. Splash with a hollow thunk and then silence. Captain wasn't playing nice, any more.

If he ever had.

"You might never make it out of here alive," Truqtok blustered.

"Ha," Captain's laugh was a rusty razor blade. "Unless you have another twenty-three goons to go with the group in here, I'm not all that worried."

"You think you can kill all of us?"

"No," Valentinian Tarasicodissa's voice turned into the single scariest thing Bayjy had ever imagined, let alone heard. "I figure we'll only kill eighteen before you get us all. Unless we get lucky. And we might. Maybe you all should have a quick vote and determine which five get to maybe escape this room alive? I'm all set to start killing the rest of your punks."

Dead silence. Or silence of death. Folks doing math in their heads for the first time since they told their teachers, way back when, that they didn't need no fancy book learning 'cause they were gonna go off and be pirate bad-asses.

"But I also recognize that I'm not staying," Captain dropped the other shoe with a perfect beat. "Planetary government should be compensated for the value of the stuff I plan to loot. And I'm not really in the mood to figure out who the legitimate government is, so I could see hauling a chunk of that gear up here and letting you make sure that it gets converted to cash and all the proper fees and such get paid to whoever should get them. I'm a businessman."

Sure, and I'm a princess, Captain. Queen of Thrika in disguise, learning about how all the little people live.

Some of the fool pirates around her looked like they might need a chiropractor after all the whiplash snapping their silly asses back and forth. Stick. Carrot. You pick.

"Big words," Truqtok's growl sounded more like a purse dog yapping now, after Captain laid the smack-down on these people.

"You want to come watch, send folks to three degrees north, seventeen degrees west and tell them to stay out of my way so they don't set off any of the traps and assassin droids the Urlan left behind to guard the place," Captain's voice sounded amenable again. "I've got specialists in disarming those sort of systems, and you don't."

Bayjy stole a glance and caught Lawyer-dude whispering in Boss-dude's ear.

"Very well, Captain," Truqtok said after a moment.

Butler used to get that gleam in his eyes when he was about to screw someone. Bayjy just lifted the plasma rifle and pointed it at the nearest goon's face before any of the shits on this side of the chamber could react.

They might draw guns now, buddy, but you're gonna be eating through a straw for a while, as your face heals.

More murmuring, but nobody was dumb enough to provoke her wrath.

"Enough," Truqtok bellowed over his anxious goons. "Captain, I will send a team to observe."

"We plan to depart in three days," Captain replied. "I have some more supplies coming, and then I'll need to break out all the heavy gear from cold storage and test it while we're close to a depot for repair parts."

"Until then," Truqtok snarled.

"Until then," Captain agreed. "Kyriaki?"

Bayjy glanced back to see Kyrie leading the reverse, so she chilled until Big Guy was in motion and walked away, eyes scanning left and right in case anybody got frisky.

She was the last to emerge from the darkness, but something had stopped the rest short, still on the porch.

Bayjy stepped to one side so she could see around Big Guy. She was just outside the front door, so maybe they couldn't rush her.

Some asshole was standing in the back of their truck, with the twin pulsar cannon pointed right at the team.

Oh, so very not good.

"Drop your weapons," the asshole in the truck yelled.

Bayjy imagined she could see eternity up those barrels.

Before she could even blink, Kyrie shot the guy right between the eyes with her assault pulsar. Three shot burst. Face shattered.

All hell broke loose.

Bayjy had enough presence of mind to turn around and just fire wildly into the hallway behind her as fast as the weapon could cycle. Plasma rifle was not a precision weapon. It fired a ball of plasma in a magnetic shell. Hit like a fist, with second degree burns if it got skin.

Actually, hit like a medicine ball. Nearest dude got it in the chest and staggered sideways, taking out one behind him and one beside. The rest were suddenly stumbling over bodies down front.

People behind her opened fire into the darkness as the plasma rifle cycled a second pulse off.

"Move," a voice commanded and a hand on her shoulder shoved her to the side, behind the stone facing of the door lintel.

She kipped her butt up against the cold stone and watched Captain drop to the ground. Big Dude and Glaxu were already hugging dirt.

Flash of light followed by a hammerblow of sound. The universe ending, maybe.

A second one, so fast she thought maybe it was an echo, until a pistol came twirling in the air out of the building like a lazy bird escaping.

Then Kyrie opened up with the twin pulse cannon.

Bayjy had seen her test fire it into a cliff. Loud and violent, like a Glaxu-sized woodpecker hunting for bugs.

The cool stone up against her butt began to vibrate in tune with the chick in the turret. Bayjy was nearly blind already, and the strobe of the guns firing right by her threatened to finish the job.

She ducked low and moved further to her left, looking for anything moving that might be a threat to Kyrie's blind side.

Another thunderbolt erupted from the building, and then Captain was up and in motion.

Bayjy kept up as they got to the truck. She stayed facing aft firing the odd shot while Captain powered things up and Kyrie went Goddess of Fiery Death on the building.

Weight shift as Big Guy and Glaxu mounted up, and then Captain was backing away from the smoking building.

Bayjy could see nothing behind them except open desert scrub as they moved, but she kept her section of the battlefield covered, at least until they were back a long ways and the truck dropped to the ground again.

The twin pulsar cannon had barely wavered in its monotonous chattering.

"You trying to bring the walls down?" Captain yelled over the noise of the generator, the cannon, the repulsors, and the evening breeze.

Kyrie ignored everyone and continued to hose the place with energy. Pulsar was good for as long as you had a generator attached, unlike an ammunition-driven weapon such as her plasma rifle.

"Succeeding," Killer-babe called back.

Bayjy had to look.

Damn, you *could* chunk a wall apart, if it wasn't reinforced for this sort of abuse. Part of the roof was already down on the south wing, where the scorch marks on the remaining parts of the wall suggested that a sniper had appeared in a window. Or some idiot wondering what all the noise outside was.

Same thing in the current circumstances.

Something exploded inside, flashing a whoof of flames and pressure out of gaps.

Kyriaki took her hands off the trigger housing finally and smiled at everyone.

"Now you see why I wanted the twin pulsar cannon, and not something lighter," she grinned.

Bayjy watched something flammable inside the building catch with an oily, black smoke. Probably was going to smell like pork soon.

Long pork.

Hopefully, the winds would carry the smell out into the desert and summon vultures and salvagers, and they could slip away.

Captain laughed and slipped the truck into motion.

"How did you know he wouldn't shoot?" Bayjy turned to Kyrie and asked.

She watched the woman pop a part off of the housing and hold it out like a birthday present.

"Because I had the fire-control safety in my pocket," Killer-babe laughed. "The rest of those morons expected that we'd be frozen with fear and they could come out and surround us."

"Huh," Bayjy grinned back at her. "Valentinian, was any of what you said back there true?"

"Only the part where we'd take down at least eighteen of them before they got us," Captain said as he drove back around the city through some of the flatlands. "You weren't looking to see that I had a detonator in my off-hand when Truqtok started getting pissy. He'd have gotten that right in his lap and he knew it."

"Are all of your parties this entertaining?" Glaxu asked as he tucked his pistol back into his holster and grabbed on to the rails.

"Oh no," Bayjy couldn't resist. "Sometimes we

leave our victims alive to appreciate that they should not mess with Captain Tarasicodissa."

The rest laughed along with her, but *that* was the truth. She just hoped that Butler Vidy-Wooders lived a long, angry life remembering the day that she broke into his ship and stole all her gear back, before turning the heat up to forty-five and breaking the temperature controls.

THE BRIDGE of *Dominion-427* was configured for Important People demanding to be present with an Important Opinion. Athanasia had generally left the captain to run his own ship without her interference, but today was too critical to leave to the amateur politicians of the Armada.

So she was present in a seat off to one side, above and slightly behind the captain as he in turn oversaw his crew preparing to back away from the station. She was dressed in black. It always seemed to center her mind into darker paths when she abandoned the white robes of the Ambassadors, or the gray of the Household.

Stephaneria had taken up a seat to one side, close enough to Athanasia to touch her hand, but with a seat between them. She was also in black, a tight outfit that showed off the long, leanness of her whippet body. The woman looked at least a decade younger over the last week, only barely approaching forty, perhaps, rather than having it long since passed and receding.

Revenge was always a good way to keep you young. Athanasia could speak to that.

"Ambassador, we're ready to depart," the captain announced in a polite, careful tone.

"Has Vidy-Wooders acknowledged?" she asked.

"He has not," the captain nodded. "We are unsure if he is currently ready to depart, in spite of your schedule."

"Ignore him then," Athanasia ordered. "He knows where we are going. If he chooses not to follow, or proves incompetent, I'll just have to find other help."

"Other help, Ambassador?"

The captain turned to her now with the first honest emotion she could remember ever seeing on his face. Granted, she had a hard time remembering what he even looked like until he walked into a room but still. Honest confusion.

Athanasia reached out a hand and let Stephaneria grasp it. Felt the woman pulse with suppressed energy that she had apparently been bottling up for years, perhaps decades, looking for an outlet. Another one of Athanasia's tools for when she caught up to the man known now as Dave Hall.

And entertainment until then.

"Once we reach Kryuome, Captain, I intend to begin the process of locating a new vessel and hiring a crew for it," she said loud enough that ears along the front half of the chamber twitched. "The Dominion never intended for you to spend eternity chasing our prey. Once they were out of Laurentian space, technically there is nothing we can do."

"Acknowledged, Ambassador," the man was hedging his bets.

"So I'll need to turn pirate, out in Wildspace," Athanasia announced for the first time to anyone other than Stephaneria. "Members of this crew who choose to remain will be given preference of position, while the rest of you will be sent back to the Dominion with my final report."

She studied the man now. Saw an actual human threaten to emerge from that colorless shell he had surrounded himself with. Probably afraid that he might be forced to end up in a situation like Stephaneria had chosen to occupy.

"Are you sure that is the wisest course of actions, madam?" he managed to get out without sounding condescending or drunk.

She had to give him points for that much.

"Captain, I intend to chase Dave Hall through the very gates of hell, if that's what it takes to get my revenge," she let the snarl fill the bridge. "I do not *require* that the rest of you be forced to attend me when we get there. Now, back away from the station and come around to the pursuit course I have given you."

"Immediately," he said, snapping to and turning to the rest of his bewildered crew. "Pilot, unlock and disengage. Back away as you have clearance and prepare to come about."

Athanasia looked over at the hungry rage slowly consuming Stephaneria's soul and wondered if that was what others saw when they looked at her. Probably. But these fools had never been more than meaningless cogs in the giant machine known as The Dominion.

She had been the wife of the Dominator himself. Head of the personal Household. One of the powers of the government, along with top officials of the Solar Party.

And none of that meant anything now. Gone, like the morning dew as the sun burned off even the memories of the dawn.

The new Dominator would never welcome her back. Probably just have her killed as an embarrassing memory of how he came to power if she proved to be an annoyance. At best, shuffle her off to a museum.

At least they had given her enough money to do this the right way. Buy a secondhand warship. Hire a crew.

Disappear into Wildspace chasing Dave Hall down.

And kill him.

The ship lurched solidly as the bolts holding it to the station retracted. Engines and gyros hummed as they went to work.

And if Butler Vidy-Wooders proved to be too little of a man to help her, then she would just have to find others.

There was a whole galaxy out there that had never learned to fear the Dominion.

At least, not yet.

[20]

GLAXU

GLAXU SQUATTED at the inner edge of the rear hatch of *Outermost* as the two cramped humans worked on his warp systems. Part of him wanted to be outside, guarding the landing zone, but the tallest human, Hall, and the lethal brunette, Apokapes, had that situation well in hand.

He had never encountered a ground weapon like a twin pulsar cannon before today, so it had been something of a shock to watch it shatter a building. *Outermost* would likely be at significant risk in a low-level attack pass. Still, they were safe for now.

The building had caught fire and then collapsed within an hour. Very few survivors had been visible in the telescopic view of his goggles, but that may have just meant that they escaped in the smoke and confusion.

Thus the two guards, on the off chance that the human locals were able to rally themselves and foment an attack. He could always take off in *Outermost*, even with the warp systems off-line, and engage ground targets, as long as he was careful about heavy defensive weapons.

"Glaxu, explain this to me again?" the oddly-colored human woman, Bayjy, asked.

They were all oddly colored, but most of them were some variation on a pink/brown spectrum, so close enough to Mondi colors. This woman was a shadowed lavender. And lacking head fur, but she still had a communicative face, when you paid attention to the skin around her eyes and jaw. Bayjy and Captain Tarasicodissa were hampered as they worked, in meter-twenty-five tall, square hallways better suited to a Mondi than a human.

"Which part?" he shifted around to look inward again.

"The Southern Chain," she replied. "Want to make sure I understand it. You actually link warpbubbles?"

"Correct," Glaxu nodded. "My kind flew south for the winter on our homeworld in the distant, forgotten past. Once we became more civilized, the migratory instinct remained intact, so we followed hospitable climes as we needed. That went into space with us. Each fightership in the nest is piloted by an individual crew member. When the lead initiates the system, each wing locks in sequentially, until the entire nest is in formation, and then we all push."

"Push?" Captain Tarasicodissa, Valentinian, asked. He might have sounded shocked, if Glaxu understood humans well enough.

"Push," Glaxu agreed. "The result is a larger warpbubble than human vessels generate, as I understand it, as well as being arrow-shaped, and thus sliding through warpspace faster."

"Huh," the human commander grunted. "Well, to test it, you might have to push *Longshot Hypothesis*, so we can see what the improvement is."

"Arrow-shaped?" Bayjy confirmed. "Slanted back at about sixty degrees?"

"Correct, Bayjy," Glaxu nodded to the woman in the engine well itself.

"Okay, so I think I see what failed," she turned and looked down into the hole, carefully keeping her head out of the way of the overhead light she had affixed to the outer hull. "You lost a part of a bracket at some point. It slid a little, and started rubbing against another piece that was never intended to be load-bearing. It failed just as you were ramping up to run and threw things out of alignment. Why didn't your nest come back for you?"

"I suspect it was because I had voted to remain in human-dominated space," Glaxu shrugged. "Rather vociferously, at that. They may have decided that I had chosen to remain, and so they might have thought they were honoring my wishes. Next time I shall be more clear about acceding to my group's decisions, if I manage to find my nest again."

"Valentinian, I need a powertorque and those needlenose pliers with the curve at the end," Bayjy said. "Glaxu, I might not be able to get this part out in one piece, so we may have to open an outside panel and lower it that way. Can you find the right panel and open it? Oh, and put a big blanket below, in case we drop anything. Don't want to have to clean sand out of delicate electronics."

"Right away, madam," Glaxu withdrew and circled under the fightership.

Looking at his vessel, it was only the slightest bit

longer than the truck Valentinian had bought, parked beside it, and not as wide, at least with the wings fully retracted in ground mode.

Apokapes nodded to him as he emerged and counted panels, finding the one he wanted before he pulled a solid tarp from a box and stretching it over the stone and sand.

Glaxu wondered about the so-called salvage task that Valentinian and his crew had chosen. The one that originally brought them to Kryuome. He had not asked, and they had not volunteered, but he rather liked these humans.

That they shared the same, lethal disdain for Truqtok and his people just reinforced that. Idly, he wondered if perhaps they were in the market to expand their nest. He had no other pressing matters, at least until he chose to go back to better-known zones.

And they were willing to help a relative stranger in need. One not even remotely related to their kind. That also spoke well of them.

He shrugged to himself and tapped on the outside of the panel.

"Bayjy, are you prepared for this to open?" he yelled.

"Go ahead," her muffled voice echoed back.

Glaxu opened the panel and let it slide out of his way, revealing the underside of the warp harness. A bolt fell suddenly and landed on the blanket. He caught it automatically with his right foot as it bounced up again.

"That's why the blanket's there, Glaxu." Bayjy laughed. "Hate to chase things like that down snake holes."

He set it off to one side, thought about it, and put it into one of his pouches so he didn't knock it out of sight accidentally.

"How may I assist?" he squatted under the nacelle and met her eyes above him.

"Got a piece here that would be easier to lower than lift," she said. "But I'm not sure your arms are long enough?"

"In that case, hold on a moment," Glaxu grinned.

He rolled sideways and rested both feet on the inside of the lip.

"Much easier this way," he matched her grin.

"Huh. Sure."

Carefully, she lowered a short length of steel pipe with brackets and wires. Zygodactyl toes were perfect to capture and lower it. For a human, it would be like having eight opposable thumbs at once.

The section was heavy, but not overbearing. He lowered it to the blanket and let go once he was sure it would not roll away.

Standing, he met Bayjy and Valentinian, just emerging from their burrow into the bright moonlight and side lighting off of *Longshot Hypothesis*.

"Neat trick," Bayjy smiled. "I'd suffer frostbite most of the time, though, if I ran around with bare feet like that."

She knelt and Glaxu moved around to one side, opposite Valentinian.

"Here," she said, pointing to a bracket that had sheared. And then a second spot worn bright. "And here. New strap and maybe some spot welds, then we should probably do the same thing on the good side. And tell your kin when you get home how to improve the design."

"I will do so," Glaxu said gravely.

"But?" Valentinian perked up.

Had he caught the underlying tones? Were humans that perceptive? Fascinating.

"But I am not sure when I will next see my old nest," Glaxu said. "They could have gone anywhere once they reached Loniea. It was nothing more than a stopover point. Were they coming to look for me, they would have been here weeks ago, so at this point I suspect I am an orphan."

"Can your ship get you home without the Southern Chain?" Valentinian asked.

It was a most poignant, and also most keen observation.

"It can," Glaxu replied. "Much slower, without everyone pushing, but that just means more stops to take on supplies, and perhaps see the galaxy."

"I'm sensing some level of discontent with that outcome," Valentinian's predator eyes bored in.

"I have no nest," Glaxu finally admitted after a sizeable pause, to himself as well as to the others.

He did not miss the quick glance between Bayjy and Valentinian. Nor the half-smile that seemed to pass, ghost-like, across the face of the woman Apokapes.

"No nest?" Valentinian drawled.

Glaxu noted how slow and languid the man's voice got when he was suddenly someone else in a conversation. The captain was some form of intellectual and social chameleon.

"Correct," Glaxu nodded. "Mondi Nests are

generally a second clan for all members, providing a social structure when far from home."

"And your nickname is *Farther*?" Valentinian asked/drawled.

"*Farther*," he agreed. "I have apparently outrun my kind. At least in this instance."

"That is an interesting conundrum," Valentinian noted. "Let's get your ship fixed first, though."

Glaxu smiled as well as his sudden melancholy would allow. At least he would be free to escape the lunatic bipeds of this planet. Where he might find a higher level of civilized discourse remained to be seen, but at least he would have options.

That was all a bird could ask.

[21]
DAVE

They were having a ship's meeting in the Rec room downstairs, so that Dave could sit in the cockpit and watch the sensor readouts directly, rather than glancing occasionally at his cardreader.

Just because Truqtok's palace had been leveled and then burned to the ground was no reason to expect that *someone* wasn't pissed enough to come start trouble. Having the four of them inside in the middle of the night, while Glaxu was buttoned up in his ship, meant that they had no guns ready to shoot, but Dave could always lift off in a hurry and move to safer ground.

Of course, Vee would magically appear in the other seat the moment Dave triggered the first engines to cycle.

"Do we know anything at all about him?" Kyriaki appeared to have chosen the role of Devil's Advocate tonight.

"Far from home, and that break wasn't something he did," Bayjy replied. "Probably sheared the first piece a year ago, and that let the other piece grind. Plus, I'm from Wildspace, and I've never even seen his species."

"And his ship is armed?" Kyriaki asked.

"Yes," Vee said. "I checked that when we were poking around. Something small on the centerline, below the ship. Two more that somehow shift around with the wings as he goes into various configurations."

"He fights with his feet," Dave called back over his shoulder. "Dewclaw, or those shock bracers, depending, so guns on the wings would fit a design aesthetic."

"A what?" Bayjy called back.

"You build ships and guns to a cultural and frequently a biological note," Dave explained. "We use rifles with a trigger at the rear third, because humans have long arms and stable shoulders. Mondi have neither, but he can move quickly across the ground and strike with his feet. The gun down the middle is his beak, for quick strikes, while the bigger ones on the outside are dewclaw strikes."

Bayjy looked at him and sighed.

"Man, and I thought Mondi were weird," she said.

Dave laughed. The woman's performance was mostly for show.

"I might have learned something as a major warlord for twenty-five years, Bayjy," he teased her. "Guns and warriors fall under that rubric."

"So what do we think of the person?" Kyriaki chimed in.

"He got at least four shots off in the firefight at the door," Dave said seriously. "The pistol was in his hands before your first target realized that he was dead, Kyriaki. The first shot went downrange faster than Bayjy got her plasma ball into play. Another shot took out one of the guards on the left flank as we retreated to the truck. He might be small, but I'm pretty sure he's as deadly as any of us."

"Feel like I'm running an orphanage, some days," Valentinian opined obliquely. "Spent three years just me and Artaxerxes, now suddenly we're talking about adding a second ship and a fifth crew member."

"You don't have to," Kyriaki noted. "He's just a spacer. And he has a ship that can get him somewhere else."

"Yeah, but he's got no family, either," Bayjy countered. "Like the rest of us. And he didn't seem in any great hurry to go home, so we're alike that way as well."

"So I'm hearing two generally in favor," Valentinian said. "Kyriaki, how do you really feel about Glaxu?"

"Civilized, erudite, and lethal," she laughed. "Probably bring the tone of conversation up around here."

They all laughed, and Dave felt a small band release around his chest.

It wasn't until he had gotten out of the Dominion that he realized just how specist his home had really been. Even Variant Humanities were not welcome there, to say nothing of a Dire Ground Cuckoo, a roadrunner like the Mondi, though he would never use that term to the man's face.

As citizens of the Dominion he could have seen either Vee or Kyriaki objecting to traveling with a true alien, Bayjy notwithstanding in her divine purpleness. She was as human, as feminine as any woman he had ever known, and more so than most, his own, estranged wife included. He was glad they were able to see the person, and not the shape.

"So we think we might want to invite him to join us in the desert?" Valentinian asked formally. "As a way of gauging his fit for longer-range planning?"

"You got it," Bayjy said.

"Yes," Kyriaki agreed.

"Dave, how much do we tell him?" Vee asked.

"As little as necessary for now," Dave glanced back and locked eyes with his captain. "I'm a wanted man. A fugitive with a bounty on his head, same as the rest of you, and possibly him now, since this planet will probably throw a fit over us wiping out a nest of vipers, even if they deserved it. And that there might be enemies stalking us. That's enough to either scare him off or reveal his true colors."

"Okay, then," Valentinian said. "Bayjy, you stay up late fixing things. Dave and I will rotate watches and naps all night. Kyriaki, you're in charge of caffeine and conversation as people need it to stay on task. Questions?"

"When are we actually leaving to go salvaging?" Bayjy asked.

"Tomorrow after you buy your trunk of dried fruit, plus whatever else happens at the sooq," Valentinian's voice suddenly sounded to Dave more like one of his former Mirlivas, the brigade commanders of the Caelon Assault Cavalry. "I want to see how the locals react, so we'll be armed to the teeth and ready to drop hell on anyone giving us trouble. That clear enough?"

Dave could hear the always-irrepressible Bayjy gulp with a bit of shock, but she was still the innocent one on the crew. Hell, she'd never even killed someone herself, other than to distract them and knock them down with the plasma rifle, just before Vee's detonators and Kyriaki getting to the truck.

"Okay, I'm taking a nap now," Valentinian said. "Dinner in ninety minutes, then Dave and I will switch off. Bayjy, hopefully you'll have it done by then?"

"Gonna try, Captain."

"To work, people."

Dave listened to them get up and start moving around. He adjusted a few of the settings on the scanner, and sent a few hard pings downrange, mostly to check the state of the burning palace. It was mostly out now. There wasn't much wood around here to burn, save for wall paneling and decorations. And the fuel containers in the basement had gone off hard early on, dull thumps echoing across the desert night.

Tomorrow, the survivors would look around and probably take a vote to do something. What that was would depend on who had lived through the night, and how many people snuck off and looked for alternate employment.

And who might decide to commit suicide tomorrow when Dave and his friends returned.

HE WAS DRIVING, because he was in charge. Valentinian was willing to admit to a certain degree of being a control freak. His parameters were just wider than most people like him. As long as things stayed with certain bounds, he could relax some.

That meant Kyriaki with the turret. Dave with his sniper rifle. Bayjy with the plasma rifle, and Glaxu with a petite weapon similar to a shock pistol, plus those shock bracers on his dewclaws.

Valentinian had gone into the armory for more detonators before they left this morning. He had three and the other three each had one, just in case. Glaxu would just have to feel left out for today if he noticed. At least until they knew which way the little birdman would jump in a crisis.

Another crisis.

The city was quiet, but the sun was only thirty minutes above the horizon now. The humans that stayed up all night had gone to bed, unless they were intent on making trouble. The natives were slow setting up their sooq, but that might be the excitement last night.

He did drive at a restrained rate this morning. Circled off the plateau a whole new direction and went around some nearby hills to come into town from the east, with the sun at his back and in the eyes of anyone feeling obstreperous.

Let the locals react to him coming into town in their own way.

He hadn't been here long enough to know the species breakdown in the region, but it felt about even, from what he'd seen. Of course, he and his crew had done a significant amount of damage to that equation last night. Someone might be upset.

And the natives might vote him a medal, because Valentinian had the feeling that Truqtok hadn't been the most popular person in town. Gut instinct, you know.

People in the roadway froze as the truck approached, then scurried madly for cover, like Kyriaki was going to open fire. Someone else would have to fire first, but he had no doubts that she'd return the favor one hundred-fold at the slightest provocation.

The main road was empty by the time he got to the edge of the market square. There was a huge spot where he just settled and hopped out of the vehicle, one step behind everyone but Kyriaki.

Since everyone else was armed to the teeth and openly carrying a weapon of some sort, Valentinian just walked. He could always quick-draw if he had to, once he knew where the ambush would arrive from.

Half the merchants they passed looked like they

wanted to dive under their tables at the first loud sound, which didn't help Valentinian's nerves one bit. The others had hard, stern faces, staring but not nodding and not greeting him.

"Bayjy," he said just loud enough to catch her ear as she walked out front. "Let's stop in and see Marduk first."

She nodded stiffly and turned that way. The merchants around them all flinched visibly as she suddenly altered course.

Marduk's small store was open. Valentinian entered alone, with the rest taking up guard positions out front.

"Good morning, Marduk," Valentinian nodded to the man. "What is the news around the sooq?"

The Jynarri grimaced sourly for a second, and then smiled a weak smile.

"A local businessman named Truqtok was apparently killed in a wild firefight inside his compound last night," Marduk said in a vague way. "Possibly a palace revolution got out of control. Many others died with him, and the palace subsequently burned enough to collapse in the darkness."

Valentinian couldn't see either of the man's hands behind the counter, so he had to assume that at least one held a weapon right now. This town had probably never seen major violence on that sort of scale. Probably just the odd mugging and occasional murder. Little things were easier to ignore as you slowly boiled a frog.

"How does your cousin feel about the outcome?" Valentinian asked obliquely. "My crew and I were all set to buy a few, last-minute things, and then head off into the desert."

"Basuk thinks that it will eventually settle back down," Marduk opined. "Other factions have considered going to rather extreme ends."

"Such as?" Valentinian twisted his shoulders just enough that he could dive behind a pillar and get to his flamer pistol in a hurry, if the need arose.

"One group advocates hunting down all of Truqtok's people and killing them like dogs," Marduk shrugged. "A more vocal splinter asks why to stop with just the bad humans, when perhaps all humans could be expunged."

"I see," Valentinian said. "And you?"

"Violence is always bad for business," Marduk shrugged again, perhaps less ambivalently. "Not everyone always recognizes that."

"Are we likely to be poisoned by the fruit Bayjy is set to buy?" Valentinian asked.

He would feel bad, dumping it in the desert on the vague risk of danger, but he would. They had enough food to last long enough to get elsewhere and resupply.

"You should be safe," Marduk said. "Few of the traders around here had any sympathy for Truqtok, but they also weren't usually the fire-breathers."

The bookseller paused in thought and rose, stepping around the counter and slipping a pistol into his pocket with a grin.

"Come," he said, slipping past Valentinian and smiling at Bayjy and the others. "Let us talk with some of my fellows."

Valentinian followed the man across the courtyard and into the rough middle of the tables.

Everyone picked a direction and kept weapons ready for violence, but the muttering around them never rose above a low rumble.

No accusations or calls for violence.

Bayjy walked up to the merchant sitting on a big trunk with a cold smile on his face. Valentinian was on her right, and Marduk her left, like an inquisition sitting in judgment of a wrong.

"Morning," she said with an amiability he could tell was forced.

She understood the tides and currents around here today.

"Greetings, pretty lady," the merchant replied. "Have fruit. Still interest?"

"Am," she said. "Can I see?"

The man rose gracefully, despite what appeared to be advanced age, and opened the trunk. Several cotton bags had been loaded into it.

Marduk walked around the table and opened the second bag, grabbing a dried fig out and inspecting it. He looked at the merchant with a hard grin.

"These are our friends," he said bluntly, taking a bite.

The merchant watched with a grin.

"Amissh and Diallak wanted to poison them, but they hate everyone," the merchant said with a low chuckle. "You owe me a dinar for the fig."

"I just wanted to make sure everyone understood where the lines needed to be drawn," Marduk said around a mouthful of chewy fruit.

"Tomorrow, maybe a week," the merchant said airily. "At some point, there will be violence. Truqtok's fools will try to assert his power. Others may try to usurp it. Amissh and Diallak will demand it be revoked entirely. Your cousin will do good business with stock on hand. But Bayjy has nothing to fear from us. Her friends give us the option of freedom from the thugs. Too bad they stopped killing when they did. Some of the rats will no doubt escape."

"Send them to me at the South Pole," Valentinian said loud enough to be widely overheard. "Three degrees north, seventeen degrees west. They can take it up with me directly, so you don't have to."

"Is true, the story?" the merchant turned now to fully face him. "Secret Urlan base left over and never found?"

"That's the story," Valentinian smiled at the man.

He noted that Marduk and the man shared a secret glance. Marduk would know the truth, but as public lies went, it would get troublemakers out of town for a while.

Who knew what might have changed by the time they made it back? If they did. Maybe they would no longer be welcome.

"Is good," the merchant decided. He bowed to Bayjy with a broad grin. "Same price, with discount for favorite customer. Forty Union Krodageni include box."

"You sure?" Bayjy asked.

"Merchant's Guild make contribution for betterment of city," he laughed harshly. Others around them joined in. "Trunk maker too stingy."

Valentinian watched the woman pull out notes and hand them to the man.

"Good," he said, pocketing them uncounted. "Now, box heavy. You have hand truck?"

"Here," Dave suddenly stepped around the table

and closed the trunk, latching it while he slid his rifle around his shoulder.

"Is heavy, human," the merchant decried. "Seventeen anath. You need help."

"No," Dave smiled at the man and picked it up, slinging it onto the shoulder opposite the rifle and holding it by a side strap.

Even Dave grunted under the weight, which Valentinian guessed to be around fifty-five kilograms, but that was a damned impressive way to get people's attention.

Jaws dropped open. Valentinian's grin was almost as big as Dave's as they departed, with Valentinian leading and Dave in the middle.

Marduk had walked with them, either as an escort or just to be friendly.

"Radio ahead before you return," Marduk said quietly. "Basuk or I will be able to let you know how safe the city is."

"Understood," Valentinian said. "Thank you."

He held out a hand and the man shook it.

"The violence was unintended," Valentinian said. "But perhaps you can make something good of it. This could be a useful base of operations for us, trading in some of the more obscure corners of Wildspace."

"And sending fools to their deaths in the polar wastes, when they seek you out?" Marduk grinned.

"Anyone like that probably has it coming," Valentinian said sharply.

"Agreed, my friend, agreed," Marduk said. "Best of luck on your mission."

He departed and they got everything loaded into the truck.

More people were out now. And more relaxed than they had been. Troublemakers would still hide in the shadows, but a city like Meeredge might be able to contain it.

Or put it to good use.

He'd be elsewhere, trying to get rich.

SHE HAD COME to appreciate what a crooked mind the captain had, but Kyriaki was still getting used to the casual lies and misdirections that tumbled out of his mouth around strangers. Not the team. No, there, he tended to play things open and blunt, so everyone knew which way to jump when things got strange.

It was just the locals who had to translate things, if they could.

She watched over his shoulder as *Longshot Hypothesis* came out of the top of her ballistic arc and nosed back over, black skies above them, sandy planet below, and that thin strip of salmon and blue at the horizon where the atmosphere could be seen edge-on.

She and Bayjy were not quite pressed up against each other in the door to the cockpit, only because the other woman was a step behind her and looking over her shoulder.

Kyriaki was used to being a little tall for a woman, but she was a half a head shorter than

Valentinian, to say nothing of the other two. The space was a tight fit.

"*Outermost*, this is *Longshot Hypothesis*," Dave was saying into an open microphone. "Prepare for descent."

"Acknowledged, Leader," Glaxu's voice came back distinctly. "Turnover point reached."

Both ships had taken off straight up and out to the edge of the atmosphere. Kryuome didn't have the sorts of Terminal Flight Control that could track them, so once they were out of sight from the ground, they vanished.

Headed to the South Pole, supposedly.

Kyriaki wondered how many people would fall for that and come looking for them. As far as Valentinian had been able to determine, the polar regions were permanently at or below freezing and frequently covered in ice miles-thick in places. The location named had the odd benefit of sitting atop a thin spot in the crust, so magma welled up in a broad ring that made a bowl valley two hundred kilometers across almost feel pleasant, at least this time of year.

Good enough to fool you into landing and looking for a hidden, Urlan base that never existed.

Had anybody actually done their homework, they would have asked why such a base wasn't hit with bolide weapons or nuclear bombs during the war. But greed was a powerful motivating force. People would see what they wanted, on the assumption that the outsiders knew something they didn't.

And then the horizon was above them, as the ship began to drop back down into the thicker atmosphere, like a falling knife. Kryuome's broad sand belts appeared, cinnamon- and cardamom-colored.

She wanted Dave to trigger a hard scan as they dove, but that would give away too much information to anyone watching, as there were certain to be. Instead, they had to fly on instruments and eyeballs.

Somewhere, a crescent of mountains a few hundred miles long, with the points aimed at the setting sun. That geology would capture all the winds from the west and funnel them into a messy swirl of weather. But it would also channel any rain or moisture into a single spot.

On any other planet she had studied, that would be an oasis. Possibly a Capital City of whatever political entity existed, just because you could farm here easier than nearly anywhere else on the planet.

Except for the background radiation.

Valentinian's console beeped angrily until he reached out a hand and dialed the volume down.

"Target acquired," the captain said tersely.

Yes. A place where the radiation would start to damage your DNA in less than two years. Neither she nor Bayjy were interested in having children. Ever. So the risk was lesser for them. No more than for the men.

And modern medicine could undo most of the damage later, something else the natives didn't have. Hopefully none lived close enough to notice them arriving, nor come bother them later.

She had already killed enough people on this planet.

"Confirmed, Leader," Glaxu chimed in as though

he was in the room with them. "Transmitting results of a prior scan now."

Dave brought it up on the screen between the two seats, the middle of three.

Yes, the same crescent range of mountains, with fourteen of them marked in bright red. Danger. Spots where perhaps a city had been annihilated with radiation weapons, once upon a time.

Valentinian's books spent only a few paragraphs on the entire devastation. Probably to spare future generations the horrors of mass murder, even against a universally-hated species like the Urlan.

Dave muttered a profanity under his breath as he adjusted the display. Several areas turned pink in fading rings outwards from the centers of those points.

Radiation warnings for people on the ground.

Better than half of the basin looked potentially lethal in weeks, rather than years.

"Dial in on E-2," Valentinian suddenly said.

Dave looked up in surprise, but Kyriaki had spotted it, too. It stood out when you dropped those pink bullseyes on the map.

Roads. Running through some of the safer zones. As if someone knew where they were.

Dave's profanities were nothing to Bayjy's in her ear. She glanced back.

"Sorry," Bayjy blushed almost indigo.

Valentinian tapped the screen.

"Looks like a ruined city here," he said.

Kyriaki agreed. Not at the center of the basin. That had some of the worst radiation signatures. This was maybe a northern suburb, if people doing the killing had gone after downtown and a military base on the southern fronting.

"Remains of one, yes," Kyriaki spoke for the first time. "Holy relics, perhaps? Temple to fallen gods?"

It even sounded weird coming out of her mouth. Enough so that both of the men turned to her in surprise. Plus she felt Bayjy's stare on her neck.

Kyriaki felt her face crimson, but shrugged it away. These were her friends.

"Someone has to have a reason to come into the death zone," she noted. "And an understanding not to stay, so they live elsewhere. Greed would have driven them to trade things they found with the outside world, so that doesn't leave much of value here besides religion."

Valentinian nodded at her thoughtfully.

"*Outermost*, we're below the horizon from Meeredge and Soulrake," he said. "Can you check your logs for a settlement west by northwest from E-2 on your map, and then scan them from altitude? We'll be coming in at night, so no running lights until we're below fifty meters elevation, but I'd like to know where they are and how technologically advanced we might have to face."

"Stand by, Leader," the Mondi killer's voice changed.

No, not killer. He sounded more like a pirate now.

The rest of them were the killers.

"Secondary target identified. Stand by for scan," Glaxu said.

Kyriaki listened to the bridge systems chirp as the fightercraft on their flank sent a pulse of energy towards the surface.

A new image appeared on Valentinian's screen,

surrounded by all the dials and gauges of his usual flight controls.

"Population estimate two thousand, Leader," Glaxu said. "Power systems and vehicles scanned, but no long-range radio transmissions or defense systems detected at present. Settlement comparable to Soulrake in most ways. Smaller and less sophisticated than Meeredge."

"Acknowledged, *Outermost*." Valentinian replied. "Maintain course and heading. Scan them randomly twice more, just in case we accidentally woke someone up, or they are playing possum. Dave, scan for a landing zone in the southeast quadrant of E-2 or northwest F-3."

"Yes, sir," Dave said.

Kyriaki remained silent and watched the two screens, memorizing the two cities displayed: one ruined that her mind kept interpreting as a temple complex, and the other almost a fortress, with low, thick walls circling the outside and a number of vehicles parked inside.

Roads suggested that most of them ran on wheels, rather than repulsors, which made sense if they had little trade with the exterior. Simple power systems ran for a long time if you maintained them, while repulsors needed constant care.

If they came for her…

No, when they came. Yes, when. They would be on the ground, marked by huge roostertails of dust in the air. Perhaps the warlord would have a flying craft of some sort, but that just put him in the air with Glaxu.

Or up where she could see him easier than he might hide in rough, undulating terrain. None of those vehicles looked armored enough to withstand a twin pulsar cannon, if she wanted to commit some level of xenocide.

Of course, she was here as a thief and a temple robber, depending on who you asked, so there was good case to be made for her being evil.

But she'd also been a White Hat, once upon a time. Some probably considered them the very essence of evil, when you got right down to it.

[24]

BAYJY

AND NOW, the tables turn.

Bayjy smiled as *Longshot Hypothesis* came in for a feather-soft landing that just amazed her. She'd never flown with a pilot that good, in more than fifteen years since she left home. And cargo transports sure as hell weren't supposed to be that nimble, but Captain had the touch.

On the ground though, she was in charge. Kinda made up for all the other craziness she'd had to go through.

She wasn't a death-dealing, fire-breathing, killing-machine sort of person, like the others had apparently been hiding under those pleasant facades. But none of them really understood the fine art of stealing shit. And now that she had stolen all her gear back from Butler, she was in business.

Ship was down on the south east side of the place Kyrie was calling the Temple. There were schools of logic to being out of sight beyond the target, as well as being upstream. Here, someone else could get to the complex maybe before the crew realized it, as opposed to having to drive by them if they were further northwest.

Captain had split the difference by finding a nice elevation where the scanners had a good circle of clearance. Down in a hollow would hide them, blind them, and probably be the place where all the heavy metals accumulated their radiation.

Whoever had blasted this place had gone in with weapons that had an exceptionally long half-life. Kinda like salting the earth. Two thousand some years later and there were still bright spots to avoid if you didn't want to grow a third eye overnight.

"All right, my little apprentices, time to get to work," Bayjy announced as she backed into the rec room, with Kyrie grinning and following.

Captain and Big Guy finished shutting the ship down and came in, about the same time that the back door chimed. Big Guy went and let Glaxu in. Quick enough, she had everyone around the table.

"So," she grinned. "Salvage is about patience, paranoia, and scholarship. In that order. It's been here a long time already, so we're not in a hurry to get it out. Never cut corners on the checklists I've provided for everyone. We never know what is a trap set to kill folks like us, so we move methodically. Good so far?"

Four nods. She'd banged on three of them enough on the way to this planet that rich salvagers had a long-term view. Butler had never gotten his head wrapped around that, so he burned his crew, which probably torched his entire reputation in Laurentia. Especially after the stories she'd told anyone who would listen.

"Two, we're in hostile country here," Bayjy continued. "Glaxu's scans don't show if anybody over there noticed us arriving, but we don't know what the local religious schedule is like, so we have to assume that someone might show up at any moment, and thus we must be prepared to bug out on short notice. That means either we drive the truck right into the bay when we're running, or we abandon it, so let's keep things neat and open back there at all times, just in case."

She fixed Dave with a hard eye that elicited a solemn nod. He would be in charge of loading and packing things, so anything that came in had to be fit into an area taped off from where the truck went. Since they would drive the truck into the aft bay with heavy things and pull them off with an overhead crane, probably safe there, but you never, ever took things for granted.

"Three, and related," she turned to Captain and Glaxu now. "Sensors need to be set up on a schedule to ping, or we need to put some sort of tripwire laser across the far end of the valley so we get warning when someone drives over to say hello. Probably both. We don't have enough spare crew to have someone just keeping sensor watch at all times, but we have to balance that with paranoia."

"Four targeting pulses at the ground did not engender a response, Bayjy," Glaxu did something with his head feathers that probably meant he was extra serious. Bird was like that. "I can set an automated targeting program in place, but we should put out localized sensors as soon as possible."

"Agreed," Bayjy nodded. "I've got a set built we can drop in the six hours of darkness we have left right now, if we want to move. Alternatively, we wait until sunset tonight and make sure nobody happened to catch a flash of light from an engine or anything."

"I vote for now," Captain said. "Paranoia, as you said."

"Good, we'll do that," she said. "Finally, scholarship. That map got us to Kryuome. It got us to these coordinates. How much tighter can it set the search?"

"I've got two more rows of details to translate," Valentinian said. "E-2 more or less corresponds to the penultimate one, or the one above it, but I'll need sunlight and time to work out a formal grid and find the last spot."

"There you go," Bayjy announced to her little, innocent ducklings. "We'll break out the truck and set sensors on the far side of the basin on the main approach. Glaxu, you'll be our backup, on your ship, so we have your sensors immediately available plus your guns if shit gets too hot to handle."

"As you command," the little birdman nodded crisply.

Yeah, Senior Cutter. Expert on the dismantling of old warships by sneaking up on the bastards who had left things behind, and getting inside their decision curve so you could see what they would do next, and prevent it.

Bayjy didn't have to be lethal. Force was usually indicative of a failure at that point, because you always ended up destroying valuable loot.

She just had to work with an entire ruined town at this point. Possibly a religious center, so she'd have demented fervency to go with sex-crazed cannibals, but that wasn't much worse than some of the crews she had worked with previously.

"Okay, then, let's break out the gear and the big guns," Bayjy commanded. "Kyrie, there are no birds larger than hawks on this planet, so anything flying that isn't Glaxu is a target and you should just splatter it first and ask questions later. Understand?"

Gun chick nodded. She'd gone quiet and serious over the last few hours. Well, even more so than usual, which was saying something, but Bayjy figured she was just feeling the weight of expectations or something.

"Let's move, people," she rose and headed aft, right behind Glaxu. Most of her gear was in a box just waiting for Big Guy to stash in the truck.

Then they could get down to the serious business of looting.

THE SUN WAS JUST STARTING to lighten the eastern sky, beyond that sharp rim of mountaintops, as they set the last of the short-range sensors. Valentinian wasn't as confident in them as Bayjy was, but he wasn't going to say anything. There were still extra layers he could add.

Dave and Bayjy walked up and stood next to him, quietly watching.

He lifted up the goggles that let him see almost as if in daylight and glanced over.

"Time to head home?" Bayjy asked.

"Probably," Valentinian agreed. "Wondering if we should set a visual sensor on the top of that central peak and aim it at the village. Plus a second one covering the southwestern approaches."

"Don't remember anything over there," Dave offered.

"Nor do I. But if I suspected trespassers, I might circle wide so I could sneak up on them," Valentinian said. "Plus, if I'm up there, we can take a really crisp picture in daylight and I can use that to map against the sensor images we have. Or just have the camera pan down."

"Okay, but I don't have anything like that in the arsenal right now," Bayjy said.

"If you sleep all day today, you can build it tonight," he offered. "I'd like to move the ship up there under darkness anyway to place something. Like you said, I'm not in a hurry to do anything until I nail down all the approaches. If whatever it is is still here, then it's going to be either buried pretty deep, or it's in the middle of their religious ceremonies. Or both."

"We need to get gone, anyway," Bayjy said. "Sun will come over those rocks lightning fast and expose our dust plume to anyone awake, so it needs to be settled down before then."

They piled into the vehicle and Valentinian powered it up. Backing away from the sensor array Bayjy and Dave had installed, he felt more comfortable. Not safe, but less like a barbarian horde was going to come over the rise before he could get his people out safely.

Kyriaki had been wound tight. Bayjy was nervous. Even Dave was moving with greater care, so at least they understood the stakes.

Valentinian let the drive back to the ship be his time to think.

He had a treasure map he was following. Seriously.

Won it in a crooked poker game, where the Sheriff of Bohrne Station cleaned out a dumb punk en route to arresting the kid and throwing him off the station. It had gotten them to Kryuome, like Bayjy had said, once they got it translated and triangulated. Got them to this basin. Supposedly got them to a specific set of coordinates laid down two thousand years ago, at or right after the end of the Great War that saw the Urlan Empire destroyed forever. Along with several hundred other, previously-inhabited planets.

What was now called Wildspace since no government had lasted long trying to rebuild. Laurentia and the star nations that way were almost exclusively pure human and well beyond it in one direction. Glaxu and his kind were apparently from the far side somewhere. All the Variant Humanities and the descendants of the Urlan Empire were more or less centered around here.

All Valentinian wanted out of life was enough money to eventually either retire, or just not care. And to take care of all of his new friends. He trusted his gut instincts, and none of them were right now telling him to run like hell, so maybe there was something here that could get them closer to wherever it was they were supposed to be.

Other than hell, that is.

[26]
GLAXU

He had promised Bayjy not to eat any of the animals he might find around here, but Glaxu already knew how stupid that idea was. The predators would concentrate whatever poisons existed in the entire biosphere, making each step worse.

Hopefully, whatever creatures lived in that village, those that all the bipeds universally called Muties, would understand to grow crops in the cleanest soil they could, and live a vegetarian lifestyle.

He even promised himself not to look down his beak at them if they did. The alternative was that they absorbed all the radiation that their prey did, in addition to what the landscape contributed.

Mutants, indeed.

With the rest of the crew having been up all night, he and Dave Hall were trading watch shifts right now. Captain Valentinian was relaxing and probably studying maps and notes. Kyriaki and Bayjy were hopefully asleep.

For his rest period, Glaxu had needed exercise. His goggles had a radiation detector built in, however rarely used, so he could do some reasonably safe explorations in the nearby ruins while jogging. And it wasn't like the natives would probably see him as a person.

No, the bipeds would be the same as in Meeredge.

At least he had not seen any smaller creatures of his type, so the Muties of the Juxx Wastelands wouldn't default to calling him a roadrunner. Even if that was exactly what he was doing today.

Outermost was keeping watch, augmented by a triple-depth of short-range detectors. Anything approaching the edges of the basin should set off an alarm, and he agreed with Captain Valentinian that an extra set on the southwestern reach would be good, as well as up on the mountain itself, if they could find a spot flat enough for *Longshot Hypothesis*.

Glaxu had considered offering to hover near a good ledge and let someone like Dave crawl out and rappel down to set the sensors they needed. Glaxu knew that man's physical capabilities were far greater than the others, for reasons not yet disclosed.

Later, perhaps. For now, he ran.

Enjoyed the overwhelming mid-day heat in ways that perhaps only Bayjy would appreciate. Set a jogging pace so slow that perhaps a human could even keep up with him over a short distance.

The ruins were psychologically magnetic, or something. They drew him in with their ancient, alien architecture and color. So much of the surrounding terrain was a pinkish, orange-ish stone. Either the kind that the winds could carve up into sand, or a harder version that might be the remains of ancient volcanoes.

Around him, however, the buildings in this area were a different color. Almost white, in spite of long exposure to etching winds, so perhaps the marble itself was white all the way through, with just the faintest, occasional colors. Glaxu could not remember seeing this color anywhere else on the planet.

He stepped close and inspected one of the walls visually before running his tongue over it. Not concrete, so it had been cut from a mountain, rather than poured in place.

The area in best repair was a cone-shaped open field, funneling one visually down to a central point that looked like a stage. Perhaps the place where a priest would call benedictions, or stand to be seen while leading the congregation.

Glaxu had no idea what Urlan religious circumstances might have been like, to say nothing of a group of semi-barbaric humans with enough technology to manage weapons and ground vehicles, but not capable air-defense networks or village-wide lighting.

Then he noticed a pattern in the stone of the square itself where the sand had blown away. Circular, with ring sections set into the ground in blocks perhaps four meters wide and ten or so along the arc.

Sand had built up in many places, but a recent breeze or storm must have disturbed enough that his eyes could see the pattern underneath. In other places, the covering was perhaps thirty centimeters thick, all the way up to massive drifts on the west-facing walls that nearly buried some buildings.

Glaxu let his perception draw him to the right. He got a running start and flapped madly enough to make it to the roof of a two-story building and turned around to see the whole cleared area.

Yes, locals still came for religious ceremonies. He could see where vehicles with plow blades on the front regularly shoveled sand out of the way for several others to park. And then paths packed down by many centuries of feet leading to the stage at the distant end away from him, down there where all the buildings worked architecturally to draw the eye.

But the uncovered circle was clear at the top, at the round end of a teardrop, if you will. The center of the design was covered, but it looked off in ways he could not identify.

Glaxu reached into a pocket and triggered the short-range radio, once he was sure that there were no rogue transmissions.

"Captain Valentinian," he said, waiting for Leader to respond. "I have something interesting here that I think you should see, sir."

[27]
DAVE

HE'D HAD to go and admit to another previously-undisclosed element from his past, but Dave was pretty good with the others knowing about his love of architecture. Not like he was going to be constructing any more cathedrals or triumphal arches, unless something extraordinarily weird happened.

More weird than his life had been so far, at least.

He and Vee were in the suburb that held the thing everyone called a Temple, standing on a rooftop with Glaxu. Notes had been left outside their doors for Kyriaki and Bayjy, whoever woke up first, so they didn't panic when the rest of the ship was empty.

The sun overhead was just coming into the hottest part of the day, so he and Valentinian were wearing those overrobes that were pretty much standard attire on this world. And guns. You didn't go anywhere on this planet without adequate firepower.

For now, that meant he kept a rifle at hand that he

could score a kill with at four kilometers on a calm day.

And he had admitted to Vee the truth about his architectural fascination and background. A Dominator had years, bubbled up inside the cocoon of the Household. Combat training was a daily thing, but it still only filled half the day. Meetings and politics were the other half, but Dave Hall had always been able to survive on four to five hours sleep, so he had several more hours in the dead of night to read.

"What do you see?" Valentinian asked without taking his eyes off the plaza below them.

"Without shifting all the sand and uncovering the rest of the design, I see an orbital map, but I can't tell if it is this system or the Urlan Homeworld," Dave replied. "Those would be my two guesses blind, but we must presume that the natives will notice someone desecrating their Holy Ground."

"Thought you'd say that," Vee noted. "Been looking at my treasure map. Those last two sets of coordinates didn't make any sense, because it looks like they suddenly want me to travel to another solar system and visit a different planet."

"Or one whose map is here, Captain?" Glaxu looked up from his studies. "I can confirm that the thing displayed beneath us is not Kryuome's system, at least as it exists today. Perhaps how it was before the orbits were altered, but I would have to uncover more and study ancient stellar records in that case."

Vee grunted a profanity under his breath.

Dave watched him hold out a hand and look down it like the barrel of a rifle, pointed at the distant stage, and then the buildings at the round end of the space.

"Got an idea," he said, turning and heading back to the stairwell that they had climbed.

Dave followed the other two down into the building to the ground floor, where the desert truck had been parked indoors, nose out, in what might have been a loading dock in ancient times.

Vee went out the front into the sun again as Dave glanced at his cardreader. The perimeter sensors still showed green, and no irritated or sarcastic messages from the women. All was well.

Outside, Vee and Glaxu had entered the clearing, so Dave followed, wondering if he had a cloth that could obscure all these tracks they were leaving. Of course, the truck would be just fine for that, so maybe Valentinian was planning to use the repulsors somehow. Maybe with a light blanket on the back. Something.

Again, Vee held up his arm and sighted down it. Turned in place and sighted the other way.

Dave regretted that Bayjy's gear didn't include a surveyor's transom, so he made a mental note to buy her one, next time they were someplace where it could be ordered. Nobody would carry one on hand, except maybe a pawn shop. He should look.

Vee moved a few steps.

"*Farther,*" Vee turned to Glaxu. "Can you walk an orbital circle cleanly."

"A what?" Glaxu's head feathers popped up in confusion.

Valentinian held out his other hand and pointed to the cleared spot.

"I need to be on the centerline connecting the two longest points of the clearing," he said. "At the point where the second orbital ring intersects. Without clearing a lot of sand, I need one of you to walk a circle for me."

"Silly human," Glaxu suddenly laughed. "There are tools. Dave, join me please."

Dave looked at Vee, shrugged, and followed the Mondi across the sand.

Glaxu reached into a pouch and pulled out a length of what Dave took to be silk rope. He moved Dave with one hand to stand at the center of the design and paid out rope until he got to the correct ring.

"Hold there, Dave," Glaxu called.

They were about fifty meters apart when Glaxu started walking, holding the other end of the line firmly.

Huh. Orbital distance measured by rope. Damned smart trick.

Quickly, Glaxu described a quarter-arc of the circle and met Vee at a spot that the Mondi scratched into the packed sand with his toes.

"Thank you, Dave."

Dave laughed and let go of the line as he walked back to the others.

By the time he was there, Vee had started shoveling sand out of the way with his hands, and Glaxu with one foot, like a giant chicken scratching for bugs.

Not that Dave would ever say that out loud. He suspected comparisons to a chicken would be even more insulting that calling him a roadrunner, as Glaxu had warned them all earlier.

But he could help, setting his cardreader to one side open so he could see the screen. He stripped off his outer robe and used it to protect his rifle against grit, before getting down on his knees and digging.

The sand was only about forty centimeters deep here, and not packed that hard. About the consistency of that first good snow, where it was wet enough to stick and make good balls, but not later when it froze into hardened concrete layers.

"Found it," Dave said, leaning back so the others could turn.

The ring, if he was spaced right, with a large, green circle that probably represented a planet, given the symbolism present.

Glaxu reached a toe and scratched delicately around the green stone, revealing that it appeared to be a sphere, inset beneath a metal ring, rather than a disk.

"Yup, that's the penultimate set of coordinates," Valentinian said with a level of awe in his voice Dave wasn't sure he'd ever heard before. "The planet rotates clockwise as the sun rises."

Glaxu gripped at the stone with a foot, but was unable to move it.

"Perhaps your strength is sufficient, Dave?" the Mondi looked up after a few moments.

Dave leaned down and braced a hand so he could get his nose right down tight and study the engineering involved.

"Going to need a chisel-tipped screwdriver," he said, mostly to himself, cursing at having to go back and get one from the truck.

Except Glaxu pulled one out of a pouch,

telescoped it much like Dave's sword, and handed it to him.

"Like this?" he grinned.

Dave grinned back and set it into one of the grooves he could see once he brushed away some sand and gave it a good blow to clean it. He leaned into the notch, but was unable to get a grip on the ring, although he could see what it needed.

After several tries, he gave up and grabbed his cardreader. Security still intact everywhere. Women still asleep.

He snapped a picture of the stone from several directions, including directly overhead.

"I'm going to have to build the right tool," Dave looked up at the others. "I can see it in my head, but this thing is on tight."

"Okay, back to the ship," Vee nodded. "We'll bring the others and maybe do this in the middle of the night where it's cool enough to annoy Bayjy."

Dave chuckled. She would demand to be here, anyway, since this was salvager work of the best kind. Buried treasure. Literally.

"Tracks?" Dave said as he rose.

Vee looked around and grimaced.

"Yeah, we need to half-bury this hole and then make it look like nobody has been here."

"I've got it," Dave laughed. "You go ahead and I'll be along."

They moved and Dave shoveled some sand into the hole with his boot. Then he dumped a double handful of sand on the hem of the robe when he picked up his rifle and hauled it behind him. Not ideal for wiping out tracks, but it did at least obscure them some. Hopefully, there would be wind later to finish the job.

Because they might actually be sitting on top of the treasure that had carried them clear across Wildspace.

He just wondered what could have been important enough to bury out here.

[28]

KYRIAKI

SHE HAD SLEPT, recovered, and woken to the sound of Valentinian and Dave tromping through the hallways, after Glaxu apparently made some earth-shattering discovery. Kyriaki didn't feel like heading aft to watch Dave and Bayjy bash metal in the shop, so she went forward to where Valentinian was keeping the sensors company in the cockpit.

He looked ragged. Worn. Like the man from the proverbs pulled though a knothole in a fence.

Kyriaki had a mug of strong coffee in her hand as she slid into Dave's usual seat on the right.

"Gods, that smells good," Valentinian sniffed.

"Want me to make you one?" she offered carefully.

Everything they did was careful. Dancing eternally around the topic without ever actually touching. She wondered if they ever would, or just lie awake at night thinking about it.

"No, but thank you," he said with an exhausted

172

nod. "I need to sleep later. Or at least nap. Caffeine right now and I'll end up too wired to sleep."

"So what did you find?" she asked. "I only got part of it from the boys as they grabbed Bayjy and her sandwich and went to work."

"The map gets us to this system," Valentinian ran a hand down his face like a wet rag. At least some of the exhaustion went with it, because his eyes were brighter when he looked up at her. "Then there was a stack of coordinates down the side that walked you through a set of waypoints."

"But?" she asked.

She'd heard him talk about those last two rows. How they made no sense in any context he could identify. Apparently Glaxu had found the key?

"The end of it sounded like I was supposed to leave and visit some other planet, circling that world clockwise to find the treasure," he sighed. "I hate riddles, but damned if every person who makes a treasure map doesn't want to show off some level of literary snobbery."

"So what happened while I was asleep?" She took another sip and watched him. It was excellent coffee that Bayjy had found for them at a previous stop. Might as well enjoy it.

"Glaxu found a piece of art in town," Valentinian replied. "A system map about two hundred meters across, half buried under the sand, but slightly uncovered by winds and age."

"Seriously?" Kyriaki felt her eyebrows climb. No wonder he hated riddles.

"Yeah," he nodded. "We traced it, dug in the right place, and found a planet represented as a sphere set in the stone. Dave and Glaxu think that they can build a key that will pull the casing open. What happens at that point is anyone's guess."

"Boobytrap?" she asked grimly.

Bayjy had talked about some of the things people did when they wanted to hide stuff, and maybe kill the person coming for it later. Some people were just assholes.

"Maybe," he said. "But it's supposedly been two thousand years since the map was laid down. I'm pretty safe assuming anything electronic that was on has probably burned out by now. Systems might have been turned off and survived, but that just means we listen to Bayjy and approach everything with sufficient paranoia."

"This was an Urlan world, right?" she asked "The so-called Overlords of the Galaxy when they were in charge of this sector?"

"Correct," he nodded. "Possibly one of their more important planets, given that someone actually went to the effort to knock it out of orbit, however little, during the late stages."

"What do you hope to find?"

"Treasure," Valentinian shrugged. "Anything that old will be worth money. I don't really care if we have to deal with the Urlan, wherever we can find any. The only real issue will be the need to steer clear of *Hard Bargain* and Captain Vidy-Wooders. I'm guessing he might be angry for a while."

Kyriaki couldn't help but grin. It has been an awesome practical joke she and Bayjy had played on the man.

"Long term?" she pressed.

They had all sort of fallen into the current situation as the best of a set of bad choices.

Valentinian had been secretly maneuvered into hiring Dave, but the former Dominator had originally been intending to quietly quit at the end of six months or so and disappear.

That would have worked, too, except for one of the Dominion Security Bureau's Inspectors looking too closely at the various stories and deciding they didn't add up. Which had led Kyriaki to chase the two men to Tartarus, and then let them go when she could have arrested them and been a hero.

Then it was her turn to flee justice, one step ahead of Dave's ex-wife, who was probably still chasing them.

Bayjy was the only innocent one here, but she had nowhere to go, same as Glaxu. With the added element of guilt by association and knowledge other people would kill her for.

So they had something like a semi-dysfunctional family, at least for a while.

"I have no idea what tomorrow will be, Kyriaki," Valentinian's eyes turned serious. "Let alone a year from now, or a decade. Back when I was just a cargo transport, I would have said that I'd have enough money in a decade to either retire completely, or start a shipping company and live like a magnate for the rest of my life. Now I'm an outlaw, and I can't offer even that much possibility."

"What happens if you do strike it rich here?" she leaned forward a little. "If we do? If there is enough money that all of us could retire?"

"Hopefully Dave could find a place to run to and relax," he sighed. "Bayjy could afford to buy her own ship and go into business, rather than working for me or someone else. Glaxu can get home, or wherever *Farther* ends up being."

She noted that he left it there. Maybe he had run out of words. Maybe he just didn't want to say anything to drive her one way or the other, unsure what she wanted.

What did she want?

Once upon a time, to be the best agent the White Hats had. An Ambassador of the Dominion Security Bureau. A cop stopping bad guys and saving the Dominion itself.

She had sacrificed all that when Valentinian Tarasicodissa turned her head and then her mind. It no longer made her as angry, but she had at least made peace with herself over the attraction she could no longer deny.

And he didn't seem to deny it, either. It was like electricity in the air, from time to time. They would look at each other and a magnetic pull would start.

"What about us?" she finally asked when she realized he was waiting for her to say something.

He paused. She could see the wheels turn in his head, but it wasn't so he could find the right lie to tell her. Trying to find the right words.

It dawned on her as she studied his face that Valentinian was younger than she. Three years, but they felt like an eternity.

But he was also far older in other ways. She had gone straight from school to duty. He had intended to do the same, but had then been kicked out of Gymnasia Dominia before he had the chance to become an officer of the Dominion Armada. For the last several years, Valentinian had been forced to survive on his wits and his charm, while she could rely on duty.

Kyriaki Apokapes could not think of someone less likely to draw her eye than a bad boy from the wrong side of the tracks.

And yet…

He had stopped breathing. She registered that because she had as well.

Poised.

She wanted to tell him to forget that question, but it had been asked. It would hang between them until there was an answer, gnawing at both of them.

"What do you want?" he asked.

That was the bullseye question. The one that always struck her like a punch to the stomach.

The reason she would lie awake at night, unable to sleep.

What did she want? She had no idea.

No, that wasn't true, as soon as she thought it.

"Honesty," she said aloud, echoing the word.

Valentinian nodded.

Considered.

Spoke.

"You drive me crazy," he said in a quiet voice. "With desire. With fear. Hot and cold. Some days I want to kiss you. Other days I want to run as fast away from you as this ship can fly, never once looking back."

Kyriaki nodded. She felt the same way. Almost word for word.

"Promise me you'll tell me before you run?" she asked.

Kyriaki hadn't asked much of the man before this,

other than a berth on his ship as they all ran ahead of the storm known as *The Widow*.

"I'll try," he said.

That was a better promise than grave assurances, because it was an honest one.

She wondered how he would react if she leaned in to kiss him right now. The atmosphere seemed to press her closer to him. He seemed to feel it as well.

A sudden, strident beeping on the console distracted them both like an electric shock.

He cursed and she watched the moment evaporate before she could grasp it back.

The man turned back into the hard-as-nails captain she had met that first day. The rogue with the lucky streak and the hard eyes.

He pushed several buttons on the console, cursing under his breath as she leaned back and drank some more of her coffee. Hopefully, they would circle this conversation again.

Valentinian looked up and his eyes came back from a great distance to focus on her.

"You're coming with me," he said starkly. "But it's time to run."

"What just happened?" she felt a surge of adrenaline spike her stomach.

"*Dominion*-427 just came out of warp overhead and pinged the planet for landing instructions."

[29]
GLAXU

"Let me repeat this back, so you can correct me and I can understand," Glaxu intoned gravely.

Captain Valentinian nodded.

Glaxu paused to draw a breath as the words seemed to jumble in his mouth.

"Dave Hall is not Dave Hall," he said, watching the two human men nod. "He is being pursued by a relentless, human female, ex-mate who we expect is aboard the ship overhead. Said warship is at least as well armed as *Outermost*, and contains ground combat troops in addition? That the best course of action suggested is to flee as soon as the sun sets and we can evade ground observation, with the expectation that the ship will have landed someplace like Soulrake or Meeredge and we can make the edge of the atmosphere safely. From there, flight. Am I generally correct?"

"You are," the Dave Hall impersonator answered. "*Dominion-427* is an assault courier, so it will be armored and armed."

179

"Why do we have an expectation that they will be able to find us here?" Glaxu tried to wrap his beak around that phase, silly as it was. "Have we not told the natives to seek us in the South Polar regions?"

"That was a misdirection," Captain Valentinian said. "A bluff I did not expect anyone would call. And if they did, to cause them to become even more lost. Athanasia will not, as I understand it, take long to find out about *Longshot Hypothesis* being on this planet. We may have left a trail of angry men and burning buildings in our path. Someone will direct her to Meeredge."

"So she does not find us at the South Pole," Glaxu stated, still off-balance that these utterly dangerous humans were suddenly spooked.

"She will take off and start looking for us elsewhere," Dave Hall said simply. "That ship will have good-enough sensors to find us on the ground, unless we spent several days disturbing the local desert enough to hide. That would, in turn, most likely reveal us to the natives, and draw their attention to the location we believe is the treasure. And we do not have enough supplies to outwait her patience."

"Ah," he finally understood. "*Dominion-427* would have the high watch as you attempted to climb out, and thus the ability to successfully interdict us."

"I doubt she would interdict, Glaxu," Captain Valentinian replied. "Based on stories Dave has told me, I expect her first choice would be to simply annihilate this ship with weapons fire and let the shattered remains fall back to the surface. *Longshot*

Hypothesis is extremely fast in warp, and not that bad in atmosphere, but I have no weapons or armor. *Outermost* might be able to engage her with a chance of survival, but I cannot."

Glaxu paused, trying to find a delicate, polite way to ask these people if they were all cowards and morons, but his vocabulary eluded him.

Bayjy saved him, perhaps.

"And if we run right now, we can lead her off," the purple woman said in a dark, heavy tone. "And then come back later and dig where you found something. I'd rather not have to worry about attacks from overhead and the ground as I worked."

"But you do intend to return?" Glaxu asked her, and then turned his attention on Captain Valentinian.

"Come too far to give up that easily, Glaxu," the man said with a harsh smile that Glaxu associated with anger.

Human body language was sometimes difficult to translate, especially the way the mouth and jaw moved, since the flesh was so much more flexible than a beak.

"And flight?" he asked. "Where would we turn to?"

"Chatosig," Bayjy said before anyone could interrupt her. "It's not all that far, and I maybe have some old connections I could call on. That gets us fresh consumables and puts us out of system for a few weeks or a month while she snoops around and realizes we're gone."

"What does she do when she truly loses your trail, not-Dave-Hall?" Glaxu asked.

"Hopefully, return home," Dave Hall said with a

human grimace. "At some point her crew will run up against the edge of their orders. I would have expected that already, since we are now on the far side of Wildspace from Laurentia, but she must have talked to someone at Bohrne Station to know we've come here."

"Will she give you up?" Glaxu pressed.

He had never mated, so he could not judge the pair-bond between humans. But rage seemed to be a motivating spirit that transcended species. That much appeared real.

"Probably not," Dave Hall admitted. "But without a warship, she becomes much less of a threat to us, so we can perhaps find the treasure and then reassess our future."

"I understand," Glaxu said. "Although I am sad that strafing the ship on the ground would most likely not be sufficient to destroy it before I was unacceptably damaged in turn. Captain Valentinian, I would like to cast my lot with you in flight. Take *Outermost* and form a new Southern Chain that will take you to Chatosig quickly, so that we can plan a return. As with the rest of you, I yearn to know what secret the desert may yet conceal, and would not share the benefit with the natives or the hunters. How may I serve?"

Glaxu found it enlightening and heartening that Leader still consulted each of the other team members with a silent look before he spoke. This truly was a group effort.

A nest he could look forward to joining.

"The truck is already in the cargo bay," Captain Valentinian said. "We will spend the next few hours watching for signs of trouble, but they should simply decide to land at one of the larger settlements and look for our tracks. Once darkness falls locally, and they are below the sensor horizon, we will take off quietly and head whichever direction takes us the farthest distance from their orbital path or landing zone. Then we'll test the Southern Chain as part of a human convoy."

"It is good, Captain," Glaxu decided. "I will return to *Outermost* and prepare. I look forward to seeing how we could combine our technology and skills to do something entirely new in the galaxy."

He rose from his squat and bowed serenely to each of them, starting with not-Dave-Hall and ending with Captain Valentinian.

Outside, the fierce sun was starting that long, amiable slide into reds and darkness, before the desert itself cooled off. He entered *Outermost* with a spring to his stride that had been missing for so long he had nearly forgotten it.

Preflight was rapid, as he had been expecting the possibility of discovery by ground-bound natives that he could perhaps engage with his forward guns as part of a larger fracas.

He had never visited the planetary system called Chatosig. Looking it up in his navigational gazetteer, it was a primarily-primary-export economy, at least on the planetary surface. Foodstuffs and raw materials transported to a vast ring of orbital stations that then processed things secondarily and tertiarily for transport to other worlds. A good place for a cargo transport like *Longshot Hypothesis* to visit, then.

The combined population there also represented so many shards of humanity that it took his breath away. Moreso when he might run into several species that were truly alien, and not just the genetically-engineered outcome of Urlan design laboratories.

He could find a place there later, if he chose.

But he had a nest now, hopefully. *Dominion-427* be damned.

Blaze Ward writes science fiction in the Alexandria Station universe (Jessica Keller, The Science Officer, The Story Road, etc.) as well as several other science fiction universes, such as Star Dragon, the Collective, and more. He also writes odd bits of high fantasy with swords and orcs. In addition, he is the Editor and Publisher of *Boundary Shock Quarterly Magazine*. You can find out more at his website www.blazeward.com, as well as Facebook, Goodreads, and other places.

Blaze's works are available as ebooks, paper, and audio, and can be found at a variety of online vendors. His newsletter comes out regularly, and you can also follow his blog on his website. He really enjoys interacting with fans, and looks forward to any and all questions—even ones about his books!

Never miss a release!
If you'd like to be notified of new releases, sign up
for my newsletter.

I will never spam you or use your email for nefarious purposes. You can also unsubscribe at any time.

http://www.blazeward.com/newsletter/

Connect with Blaze!

Web: www.blazeward.com
Boundary Shock Quarterly (BSQ):
https://www.boundaryshockquarterly.com/

facebook.com/KRPBlaze

goodreads.com/Blaze_Ward

bookbub.com/authors/blaze-ward

Knotted Road Press fiction specializes in dynamic writing set in mysterious, exotic locations.

Knotted Road Press non-fiction publishes autobiographies, business books, cookbooks, and how-to books with unique voices.

Knotted Road Press creates DRM-free ebooks as well as high-quality print books for readers around the world.

With authors in a variety of genres including literary, poetry, mystery, fantasy, and science fiction, Knotted Road Press has something for everyone.

Knotted Road Press
www.KnottedRoadPress.com